Resounding praise for
the incomparable western fiction of
New York Times bestselling Grand Master

ELMORE LEONARD

✫ ✫ ✫

"Leonard began his career telling western stories. He knows his way onto a horse and out of a gun fight as well as he knows the special King's English spoken by his patented, not-so-lovable urban lowlifes."

Milwaukee Journal Sentinel

"In cowboy writing, Leonard belongs in the same A-list shelf as Louis L'Amour, Owen Wister, Max Brand, and Zane Grey."

New York Daily News

"Leonard wrote westerns, very good westerns . . . the way he imagined Hemingway, his mentor, might write westerns."

Baton Rouge Sunday Advocate

"A master . . . Etching a harsh, haunting landscape with razor-sharp prose, Leonard shows in [his] brilliant stories why he has become the American poet laureate of the desperate and the bold . . . In stories that burn with passion, treachery, and hero-ism, the frontier comes vividly, magnificently to life."

Tulsa World

"[Leonard's stories] transcend the genre to work as well as any serious fiction of the era—or any era."

Chicago Tribune

Books by Elmore Leonard

Moment of Vengeance and
  Other Stories
The Complete Western
  Stories of Elmore
  Leonard
Mr. Paradise
When the Women Come
  Out to Dance
Tishomingo Blues
Pagan Babies
Be Cool
The Tonto Woman &
  Other Western Stories
Cuba Libre
Out of Sight
Riding the Rap
Pronto
Rum Punch
Maximum Bob
Get Shorty
Killshot
Freaky Deaky
Touch
Bandits

Glitz
LaBrava
Stick
Cat Chaser
Split Images
City Primeval
Gold Coast
Gunsights
The Switch
The Hunted
Unknown Man No. 89
Swag
Fifty-two Pickup
Mr. Majestyk
Forty Lashes Less One
Valdez Is Coming
The Moonshine War
The Big Bounce
Hombre
Last Stand at Saber River
Escape from Five Shadows
The Law at Randado
The Bounty Hunters

ELMORE LEONARD

Moment of Vengeance
and other stories

HarperTorch
An Imprint of HarperCollinsPublishers

◆

HARPERTORCH
An Imprint of HarperCollins*Publishers*
10 East 53rd Street
New York, New York 10022-5299

Copyright © 2006 by Elmore Leonard, Inc.
The Complete Western Stories of Elmore Leonard copyright © 2004 by Elmore Leonard, Inc.
Map designed by Jane S. Kim
Collection editor, Gregg Sutter
ISBN-13: 978-0-06-072428-3
ISBN-10: 0-06-072428-5

First HarperTorch paperback printing: July 2006

The stories contained in this volume appeared in *The Complete Western Stories of Elmore Leonard*, published in December 2004 by William Morrow, an imprint of HarperCollins Publishers.

HarperCollins®, HarperTorch™, and ◆™ are trademarks of HarperCollins Publishers Inc.

Printed in the United States of America

Visit HarperTorch on the World Wide Web at www.harpercollins.com

10 9 8 7 6 5 4 3 2 1

★ Contents ★

Map		*vii*
1	Law of the Hunted Ones	*1*
2	The Hard Way	*58*
3	Trouble at Rindo's Station	*79*
4	No Man's Guns	*129*
5	The Rancher's Lady	*153*
6	Moment of Vengeance	*176*
7	The Nagual	*202*

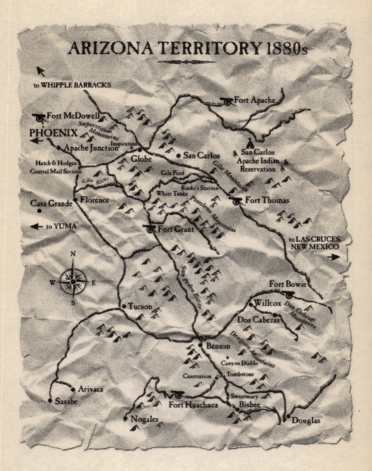

Moment of Vengeance

1

Law of the Hunted Ones

★

Chapter One

PATMAN SAW IT first. The sudden flash of sun on metal; then, on the steepness of the hillside, it was a splinter of a gleam that hung unmoving amidst the confusion of jagged rock and brush. Just a dull gleam now that meant nothing, but the first metallic flash had been enough for Virgil Patman.

He exhaled slowly, dropping his eyes from the gleam up on the slanting wall, and let his gaze drift up ahead through the narrowness, the way it would naturally. But his fists remained tight around the reins. He muttered to himself, "You damn fool." Cover was behind, a hundred feet or more, and a rifle can do a lot of pecking in a hundred feet.

The boy doesn't see it, he thought. Else he would have been shooting by now. And then other words followed in his mind. Why do you think the boy's any dumber than you are?

He shifted his hip in the saddle and turned his head halfway around. Dave Fallis was a few paces behind him and to the side. He was looking at his hands on the flat dinner-plate saddle horn, deep in thought.

Patman drew tobacco and paper from his side coat pocket and held his mount in until the boy came abreast of him.

"Don't look up too quick and don't make a sudden move," Patman said. He passed the paper along the tip of his tongue, then shaped it expertly in his bony, freckly fingers. He wasn't looking at the boy, but he could sense his head come up fast. "What did I just tell you?"

He struck a match and held it to the brown paper cigarette. His eyes were on the match and he half-mumbled with the cigarette in his mouth, "Dave, hold on to your nerve. There's a rifle pointing at us. Maybe two hundred feet ahead and almost to the top of the slope." He handed the makings across.

"Build yourself one like it was Sunday afternoon on the front porch."

Their horses moved at a slow walk close to the left side that was smooth rock and almost straight up. Here, and as far as you could see ahead, the right side slanted steeply up, gravel, rock and brush thrown violently together, to finally climb into dense pines overhead. Here and there the pines straggled down the slope. Patman watched the boy put the twisted cigarette between his lips and light it, the hand steady, up close to his face.

"When you get a chance," Patman said, "look about halfway up the slope, just this side of that hollow. You'll see a dab of yellow that's prickly pear, then go above to that rock jam and tell me what you see."

Fallis pulled his hat closer to his eyes and looked up-canyon before dragging his gaze to the slope. His face registered nothing, not even a squint with the hat brim resting on his eyebrows. A hard-boned face, tight through the cheeks and red-brown from the sun, but young and with a good mouth that looked as if it smiled most of the time, though it wasn't smiling now. His gaze lowered to the pass and he drew on the cigarette.

"Something shining up there, but I don't make out what it is," he said.

"It's a rifle, all right. We'll take for granted somebody's behind it."

"Indian?"

"Not if the piece is so clean it shines," Patman answered. "Just keep going, and watch me. We'll gamble that it's a white man—and gamble that he acts like one."

Fallis tried to keep his voice even. "What if he just shoots?" The question was hoarse with excitement. *Maybe the boy's not as scared as I am,* Patman thought. *Young and too eager to be afraid. You get old and take too damn much time doing what kept you alive when you were young. Why keep thinking of him,* he thought, *you got a hide too, you know.*

Patman answered, "If he shoots, we'll know where we stand and you can do the first thing that comes to your mind."

"Then I might let go at you," Fallis smiled, "for leading us into this jackpot."

Patman's narrow face looked stone-hard with its sad smile beneath the full mustache. "If you want to make jokes," he said, "go find someone else."

"What're we going to do, Virg?" Fallis was dead serious. It made his face look tough when he didn't smile, with the heavy cheekbones and the hard jawline beneath.

"We don't have a hell of a lot of choices," Patman said. "If we kick into a run or turn too fast, we're likely to get a bullet. You don't want to take a chance on that gent up there being the nervous type. And if we just start shooting, we haven't got anything to hide behind when he shoots back."

He heard the boy say, "We can get behind our horses."

He answered him, "I'd just as soon get shot as have to walk home. You got any objections to just going on like we don't know he's there?"

Fallis shook his head, swallowing. "Anything you say, Virg. Probably he's just out hunting turkeys. . . ." He dropped behind the older man as they edged along the smooth rock of the canyon wall until there was ten feet between their horses.

★ ★ ★

THEY RODE STIFF-BACKED, from habit, yet with an easy looseness of head and arms that described an absence of tension. Part of it was natural, again habit, and part was each trying to convince the other that he wasn't afraid. Patman and Fallis were good for each other. They had learned it through campaigning.

Now, with the tightness in their bellies, they

waited for the sound. The clop of their horses' hooves had a dull ring in the awful silence. They waited for another sound.

Both men were half expecting the heavy report of a rifle. They steeled themselves against the worst that could happen, because anything else would take care of itself. The sound of the loose rock glancing down the slope was startling, like a warning to jerk their heads to the side and up the slanting wall.

The man was standing in the spot where Patman had pointed, his rifle at aim, so that all they could see was the rifle below the hat. No face.

"Don't move a finger, or you're dead!" The voice was full and clear. The man lowered the rifle and called, "Sit still while I come down."

He turned and picked his way over the scattered rock, finally half sliding into the hollow that was behind his position. The hollow fell less steeply to the canyon floor with natural rock footholds and gnarled brush stumps to hold on to.

For a moment the man's head disappeared from view, then was there again just as suddenly. He hesitated, watching the two men below him and fifty feet back up the trail. Then he disappeared again into a deeper section of the descent.

Dave Fallis' hand darted to the holster at his hip. "Hold onto yourself!" Patman's whisper was a growl in his heavy mustache. His eyes flicked to the hollow. "He's not alone! You think he'd go out of sight if he was by himself!"

The boy's hand slid back to the saddle horn while his eyes traveled over the heights above him. Only the hot breeze moved the brush clumps.

The man moved toward them on the trail ahead with short, bowlegged steps, his face lowered close to the upraised rifle. When he was a dozen steps from Patman's horse, his head came up and he shouted, "All right!" to the heights behind them. Fallis heard Patman mumble, "I'll be damned," looking at the man with the rifle.

"Hey, Rondo!" Patman was grinning his sad smile down at the short, bowlegged man with the rifle. "What you got here, a toll you collect from anybody who goes by?" Patman laughed out, with a ring of relief to the laugh. "I saw you a ways back. Your toll box was shining in the sun." He went on laughing and put his hand in his side coat pocket.

The rifle came up full on his chest. "Keep your hand in sight!" The man's voice cut sharply.

Patman looked at him surprised. "What's the matter with you, Rondo? It's me. Virg Patman." His arm swung to his side. "This here's Dave Fallis. We rode together in the Third for the past five years."

Rondo's heavy-whiskered face stared back, the deep lines unmoving as if they had been cut into stone. The rifle was steady on Patman's chest.

"What the hell's the matter with you!" Patman repeated. "Remember me bringing you your bait for sixty days at Thomas?"

Rondo's beard separated when his mouth opened slightly. "You were on the outside, if I remember correctly."

Patman swore with a gruff howl. "You talk like I passed sentence! You damn fool, what do you think a Corporal of the Guard is—a judge?" His head turned to Fallis. "This bent-legged waddie shoots a reservation Indian, gets sixty days, then blames it on me. You remember him in the lock-up?"

"No. I guess—"

"That's right," Patman cut in. "That was before your time."

Rondo looked past the two men.

"That wasn't before my time." The voice came from behind the two men.

* * *

HE WAS SQUATTING on a hump that jutted out from the slope, just above their heads and a dozen or so feet behind them, and he looked as if he'd been sitting there all the time. When he looked at him, Fallis thought of a scavenger bird perched on the bloated roundness of a carcass.

It was his head and the thinness of his frame that gave that impression. His dark hair was cropped close to his skull, brushed forward low on his forehead and coming to a slight point above his eyebrows. The thin hair pointed down, as did the ends of a shadowy mustache that was just starting to grow, lengthening the line of his face, a face that was sallow complexioned and squinting against the brightness of the afternoon.

He jumped easily from the hump, his arms outstretched and a pistol in each hand, though he wore only one holster on his hip.

Fallis watched him open-mouthed. He wore a faded undershirt and pants tucked into knee-high boots. A string of red cotton was knotted tight to his throat above the opening of the undershirt. And with it all, the yellowish death's-head of a face. Fallis watched because he couldn't take his eyes from the man. There was a compelling arrogance about his movements and the way he held his head that made Fallis stare at him. And even with the shabbiness of his dress, it stood out. It was there in the way he held his pistols. Fallis pictured a saber-slashing captain of cavalry. Then he saw a black-bearded buccaneer.

"I remember when Rondo was in the lock-up at Fort Thomas." His voice was crisp, but low and he extra-spaced his words. "That was a good spell before you rode me to Yuma, wasn't it?"

Patman shook his head. The surprise had already left his face. He shook his head wearily as if it was all way above him. He said, "If you got any more men up there that I policed, get 'em down and let me hear it all at once." He shook his head again. "This is a real day of surprises. I can't say I ever expected to see you again, De Sana."

"Then what are you doing here?" The voice was cold-clear, but fell off at the end of the question as if he had already made up his mind why they were there.

Patman saw it right away.

It took Fallis a little longer because he had to fill in, but he understood now, looking at De Sana and then to Patman.

Patman's voice was a note higher. "You think we're looking for you?"

"I said," De Sana repeated, "then what are you doing here?"

"Hell, we're not tracking you! We were mustered out last week. We're pointing toward West Texas for a range job, or else sign for contract buffalo hunters."

De Sana stared, but didn't speak. His hands, with the revolving pistols, hung at his sides.

"What do I care if you broke out of the Territory prison?" Patman shouted it, then seemed to relax, to calm himself. "Listen," he said, "we're both mustered out. Dave here has got one hitch in, and I've got more years behind me than I like to remember. But we're out now and what the army does is its own damn business. And what you do is your business. I can forget you like that." He snapped his fingers. " 'Cause you don't mean a thing to me. And that dust-eatin' train ride from Willcox to Yuma, I can forget that too, 'cause I didn't enjoy it any more than you did even if you thought then you weren't going to make the return trip. You're as bad as Rondo here. You think 'cause I was train guard it was my fault you got sent to Yuma. Listen. I treated you square. There were some troopers would have kicked your face in just on principle."

De Sana moistened his lower lip with his tongue, idly, thinking about the past and the future at the same time. A man has to believe in something, no matter what he is. He looked at the two men on the horses and felt the weight of the pistols in his hands. There was the easy way. He looked at them watching him uneasily, waiting for him to make a move.

"Going after a range job, huh?" he said almost inaudibly.

"That's right. Or else hunt buffalo. They say the railroad's paying top rate, too," Patman added.

"How do I know," De Sana said slowly, "you won't get to the next sheriff's office and start yelling wolf."

Patman was silent as his fingers moved over his jaw. "I guess you'll have to take my word that I've got a bad memory," he said finally.

"What kind of memory has your friend got?" De Sana said, looking hard at Dave Fallis.

"You got the biggest pistols he ever saw," Patman answered.

Rondo mounted behind Patman and pointed the way up the narrow draw that climbed from the main trail about a quarter of a mile up. It branched from the pass, twisting as it climbed, but more decidedly bearing an angle back in the direction from which they had come. Rondo had laughed out at Patman's last words. The tension was off now. Since De Sana had accepted the two men, Rondo would too, and went even a step further, talking about hospitality and coffee and words like this calls for a celebration, even though the words were lost on the other three men. The words had no meaning but they filled in and lessened the tension.

★

Chapter Two

De Sana was still standing in the pass when they left, but when Fallis looked back he saw the outlaw making his way up the hollow.

When the draw reached the end of its climb they were at the top of the ridge, looking down directly to the place where they had held up. Here, the pines were thick, but farther off they scattered and thinned again as they began to stretch toward higher, rockier ground.

De Sana was standing among the trees waiting for them. He turned before they reached him and led the way through the pines. Fallis looked around curiously, feeling the uneasiness that had come over him since meeting De Sana. Then, as he looked ahead, the hut wasn't fifty feet away.

It was a low structure, flat-roofed and windowless, with rough, uneven logs chinked in with adobe mud. On one side was a lean-to where the cooking was done. A girl was hanging strips of meat from the low ceiling when they came out of the pines, and as they approached she turned with a hand on her hip, smoothing a stray wisp of hair with the other.

She watched them with open curiosity, as a small child stares at the mystery of a strange person. There was a delicateness of face and body that accentuated this, that made her look more child-like in her open sensitivity. De Sana glanced at her and she dropped her eyes and turned back to the jerked meat.

"Put the coffee on," De Sana called to her. She nodded her head without turning around. "Rondo, you take care of the mounts and get back to your nest."

Rondo opened his mouth to say something but thought better of it and tried to make his face look natural when he took the reins from the two men and led the horses across the small clearing to the corral, part of which could be seen through the pines a little way off. A three-sided lean-to squatted at one end of the small, fenced area.

"That's Rondo's," De Sana pointed to the shelter. Walking to the cabin he called to the girl again. This time she did not shake her head. Fallis thought perhaps the shoulders tensed in the faded gray dress. Still, she didn't turn around or even answer him.

The inside of the cabin was the same as the outside, rough log chinked with adobe, and a packed dirt floor. A table and two chairs, striped with cracks and gray with age, stood in the middle of the small room. In a far corner was a straw mattress. On it, a blanket was twisted in a heap. Along the opposite wall was a section of log with a board nailed to it to serve as a bench, and next to this was the cupboard: three boxes stacked one on the other. It contained a tangle of clothing, cartridge boxes and five or six bottles of whiskey.

The two men watched De Sana shove his extra pistol into a holster that hung next to the cupboard. The other was on his hip. He took a half-filled bottle from the shelf and went to the table.

"Looks like I'm just in time." Rondo was standing in the doorway, grinning, with a canteen hanging from his hand. "Give me a little fill, *jefe,* to ease sitting on that eagle's nest."

De Sana's head came up and he moved around the table threateningly, his eyes pinned on the man in the doorway. "Get back to the pass!" His hand dropped to the pistol on his hip in a natural movement. "You watch! You get paid to watch! And if you miss anything going through that pass . . ." His voice trailed off, but for a moment it shook with excitement.

"Hell, Lew. Nobody's going to find us way up here," Rondo argued half-heartedly.

Patman looked at him surprised. "Cima Quaine's

blood-dogs could track a man all the way to China."

"Aw, San Carlos's a hundred miles away. Ain't nobody going to track us that far, not even 'Pache Police."

De Sana said, "I'm not telling you again, Rondo." Rondo glanced at the hand on the pistol butt and moved out of the doorway.

But as he walked through the pines toward the canyon edge, he held the canteen up to his face and shook it a few times. He could hear the whiskey inside sloshing around sounding as if it were still a good one-third full. Rondo smiled and his mind erased the scowling yellow face. Lew De Sana could go take a whistlin' dive at the moon for all he cared.

★ ★ ★

THE GIRL'S FINGERS were crooked through the handles of the three enamel cups, and she kept her eyes lowered to the table as she set the coffeepot down with her other hand, placing the cups next to it.

"Looks good," Patman said.

She said nothing, but her eyes lifted to him briefly, then darted to the opposite side of the table where Fallis stood and then lowered just as quickly. She had turned her head slightly, enough for Fallis to see the bruise on her cheekbone. A deep blue beneath her eye that spread into a yellowish caste in the soft hollow of her cheek. There was a lifelessness in the dark eyes and perhaps fear. Fallis kept staring at the girl, seeing the utter resignation that showed in her face and was there even in the way she moved her small body. Like a person who has given up and doesn't much care what happens next. He noticed the eyes when her glance wandered to him again, dark and tired, yet with a certain hungriness in their deepness. No, it wasn't fear.

De Sana picked up the first cup as she filled it and poured a heavy shot from the bottle into it. He set the bottle down and lifted the coffee cup to his mouth. His lips moved, as if tasting, and he said, "It's cold," looking at the girl in a way that didn't need the support of other words. He turned the cup upside down and poured the dark liquid on the floor.

Fallis thought, *What a damn fool. Who's he trying to impress?* He glanced at Patman but the ex-corporal was looking at De Sana as if pouring coffee on the floor was the most normal thing in the world.

As the girl picked up the big coffeepot, her hand shook with the weight and before her other hand could close on the spout, she dropped it back on the table.

"Here, I'll give you a hand," Fallis offered. "That's a big jug."

But just as he took it from the girl's hands, he heard De Sana say, "Leave that pot alone!"

He looked at De Sana in bewilderment. "What? I just want to help her out with the coffeepot."

"She can do her own chores." De Sana's voice was unhurried. "Just put it down."

Dave Fallis felt heat rise up over his face. When he was angry, he always wondered if it showed. And sometimes, as, for instance, now, he didn't care. His heart started going faster with the rise of the heat that tingled the hair on the back of his head and made the words come to his mouth. And he had to spit the words out hard because it would make him feel better.

"Who the hell are you talking to? Do I look like somebody you can give orders to?" Fallis stopped but kept on looking at the thin, sallow face, wishing he could think of something good to say while the anger was up.

Patman moved closer to the younger man. "Slow down, Dave," he said with a laugh that sounded forced. "A man's got a right to run things like he wants in his own house."

De Sana's eyes moved from one to the other, then back to the girl and said, "What are you waiting for?" He kept his eyes on her until she passed through the doorway. Then he said, "Mister, you better have a talk with your boy."

Fallis heard Patman say, "That's just his Irish, Lew. You know, young and gets hot easy." He stared at the old cavalryman—not really old, but twice his own age—and tried to see through the sad face with the drooping mustache because he knew that wasn't Virg Patman talking, calling him by his first name as if they were old friends. What was the matter with Virg? He felt the anger draining and in its place was bewilderment. It made him feel uneasy and kind of foolish standing there, with his big hands planted on the table, trying to stare down the skeletal-looking gunman who looked at him as if he were a kid and would be just wasting his time talking. It made him madder, but the things he wanted to say sounded too loudmouth in his mind. The words seemed blustering, hot air, compared to the cold, slow-spoken words of De Sana.

Now De Sana said, "I don't care what his nationality is. But I think you better tell him the facts of life."

Fallis felt the heat again, but Patman broke in with his laugh before he could say anything.

"Hell, Lew," Patman said. "Let's get back to what we come for. Nobody meant any harm."

De Sana fingered the dark shadow of his mustache thoughtfully, and finally said, hurriedly, "Yeah. All right." Then he added, "Now that you're here, you might as well stay the night and leave in the morning. If you have any stores with you, break them out. This isn't any street mission. And remember, first light you leave."

Later, during the meal, he spoke little, occasionally answering Patman in monosyllables. He never spoke directly to Fallis and only answered Patman when he had to. Finally he pushed from the table before he had finished. He rolled a cigarette moving toward the door. "I'm going out to relieve Rondo," he said. "Don't wander off."

★ ★ ★

FALLIS WATCHED HIM walk across the clearing and when the figure disappeared into the pines he turned abruptly to Patman sitting next to him.

"What's the matter with you, Virg?"

Patman put his hand up. "Now just slow it down. You're too damn jumpy."

"Jumpy? Honest to God, Virg, you never sucked up to the first sergeant like you did to that little rooster. Back in the pass you read him out when he started jumping to conclusions. Now you're buttering up like you were scared to death."

"Wait a minute." Patman passed his fingers through his thinning hair, his elbow on the table. He looked very tired and his long face seemed to sag loosely in sadness. "If you're going to play brave, you got to pick the right time, else your bravery don't mean a damn thing. These hills are full of heroes, and nobody even knows where to plant the flowers over them. Then you come across a man fresh out of Yuma—out the hard way, too—" he added, "a man who probably shoots holes in his shadow every night and can't trust anybody because it might mean going back to an adobe cell block. He got sent there in the first place because he shot an Indian agent in a hold-up. He didn't kill him, but don't think he couldn't have—and don't think he hasn't killed before."

Patman exhaled and drew tobacco from his pocket. "You run into a man like that, a man who counts his breaths like you count your blessings, and you pick a fight because you don't like the way he treats his woman."

"A man can't get his toes stepped on and just smile," Fallis said testily.

Patman blew smoke out wearily. "Maybe your hitch in the Army was kind of a sheltered life. Brass bands and not having to think. Trailing a dust cloud that used to be Apaches isn't facing Lew De

Sana across a three foot table. I think you were lucky."

Fallis picked up his hat and walked toward the door. "We'll see," he answered.

"Wait a minute, Dave." Fallis turned in the doorway.

"Sometimes you got to pick the lesser of evils," the older man said. "Like choosing between a sore toe or lead in your belly. Remember, Dave, he's a man with a price on his head. He's spooky. And remember this. A little while ago he could have shot both of your eyes out while he was drinking his coffee."

Patience wasn't something Dave Fallis came by naturally. Standing idle ate at his nerves and made him move restlessly like a penned animal. The Army hitch had grated on him this way. Petty routines and idleness. Idleness in the barracks and idleness even in the dust-smothering parade during the hours of drill. Routine that became so much a part of you it ceased being mentally directed.

The cavalry had a remedy for the restless feeling. Four-day patrols. Four-day patrols that sometimes stretched to twenty and by it brought the ailment back with the remedy. For a saddle is a poor place for boredom, and twelve hours in it will bring the boredom back quicker than anything else, especially when the land is flat and vacant, silent but for a monotonous clop, blazing in its silence and carrying only dust and a sweat smell that clung sourly to you in the daytime and chilled you at night. Dave Fallis complained because nothing happened—because there was never any action. He was told he didn't know how lucky he was. That he didn't know what he was talking about because he was just a kid. And nothing made him madder. Damn a man who's so ignorant he holds age against you!

Now he stood in the doorway and looked out across the clearing. He leaned against the doorjamb, hooking his thumbs in his belt, and let his body go loose. The sun was there in front of him over the trees, casting a soft spread of light on the dark hillsides in the distance. Now it was a sun that you could look at without squinting or pulling down your hat brim. A sun that would be gone in less than an hour.

He saw the girl appear and move toward the lean-to at the side of the hut. She walked slowly, listlessly.

Fallis left the doorway and idled along the front of the hut after she had passed and entered the shelter. And when he ducked his head slightly and entered the low-roofed shed, the girl was busy scooping venison stew from the pot and dishing it onto one of the tin plates.

★ ★ ★

SHE TURNED QUICKLY at the sound of his step and almost brushed him as she turned, stopping, her mouth slightly open, her face lower than his, but not a foot separating them.

He was grinning when she turned, but the smile left his face as she continued to stare up at him, her mouth still parted slightly and warm looking, complementing the delicately soft lines of nose and cheekbones. The bruise was not so noticeable now, in the shadows, but its presence gave her face a look of sadness, yet adding luster to the deep brown eyes that stared without blinking.

His hands came up to grip her shoulders, pulling gently as he lowered his face to hers. She yielded against the slight pressure of his hands, drawing closer, and he saw her eyes close as her face tilted back, but as he closed his eyes he felt her shoulders jerk suddenly from his grip and in front of his face now was the smooth blackness of her hair hanging straight about her shoulders.

"Why did you do that?" Her voice was low, and with her back to him, barely audible.

Fallis said, "I haven't done anything yet," and

tried to make his voice sound light. The girl made no answer, but remained still, with her shoulder close to him.

"I'm sorry," he said. "Are you married to him?"

Her head shook from side to side in two short motions, but no sound came from her. He turned her gently, his hands again on her shoulders, and as she turned she lowered her head so he could not see her face. But he crooked a finger beneath her chin and raised it slowly to his. His hand moved from her slender chin to gently touch the bruised cheekbone.

"Why don't you leave him?" He half-whispered the words.

For a moment she remained silent and lowered her eyes from his face. Finally she said, "I would have no place to go." Her voice bore the hint of an accent.

"What's worse than living with him and getting beat like an animal?"

"He is good to me—most of the time. He is tired and nervous and doesn't know what he is doing. I remember him when he was younger and would visit my father. He smiled often then and was good to us." Her words flowed faster now, as if she was anxious to speak, voluntarily lifting her face to look into his with a pleading in her dark eyes that seemed to say, "Please believe what I say and tell me that I am right."

"My father," she went on, "worked a small farm

near Nogales which I remember as far back as I am able. He worked hard but he was not a very good farmer, and I always had the feeling that papa was sorry he had married and settled there. You see, my mother was Mexican," and she lowered her eyes as if in apology.

"One day this man rode up and asked if he may buy coffee. We had none, but he stayed and talked long with papa and they seemed to get along very well. After that he came often, maybe two three times a month and always he brought us presents and sometimes even money, which my papa took and I thought was very bad of him, even though I was only a little girl. Soon after that my mother died of sickness, and my papa took me to Tucson to live. And from that time he began going away for weeks at a time with this man and when he returned he would have money and he would be very drunk. When he would go, I prayed to the Mother of God at night because I knew what he was doing.

"Finally, he went away and did not return." Her voice carried a note of despair. "And my prayers changed to ones for the repose of his soul."

Fallis said, "I'm sorry," awkwardly, but the girl went on as if he had not spoken.

"A few months later the man returned and treated me differently." Her face colored slightly.

"He treated me older. He was kind and told me he would come back soon and take me away from Tucson to a beautiful place I would love. . . . But it was almost two years after this that the man called Rondo came to me at night and took me to the man. I had almost forgotten him. He was waiting outside of town with horses and made me go with them. I did not know him, he had changed so—his face, and even his voice. We have been here for almost two weeks, and only a few days ago I learned where he had been for the two years."

Suddenly, she pressed her face into his chest and began to cry silently, convulsively.

Fallis's arms circled the thinness of her shoulders to press her hard against his chest. He mumbled, "Don't cry," into her hair and closed his eyes hard to think of something he could say. Feeling her body shaking against his own, he could see only a smiling, dark-haired little girl looking with awe at the carefree, generous American riding into the yard with a war bag full of presents. And then the little girl standing there was no longer smiling, her cheekbone was black and blue and she carried a half-gallon coffeepot in her hands. And the carefree American became a sallow death's-head that she called only "the man."

With her face buried against his chest, she was speaking. At first he could not make out her words, incoherent with the crying, then he realized that she was repeating, "I do not like him," over and over, "I do not like him." He thought, how can she use such simple words? He lifted her head, her eyes closed, and pressed his mouth against the lips that finally stopped saying, "I do not like him."

She pushed away from him lingeringly, her face flushed, and surprised the grin from his face when she said, "Now I must get wood for in the morning."

The grin returned as he looked down at her childlike face, now so serious. He lifted the hand-ax from the wood box, and they walked across the clearing very close together.

Virgil Patman stood in the doorway and watched them dissolve into the darkness of the pines.

Well, what are you going to do? Maybe a man's not better off minding his own business. The boy looks like he's doing pretty well not minding his. But damn, he thought, he's sure making it tough! He stared out at the cold, still light of early evening and heard the voice in his mind again. You've given him a lot of advice, but you've never really done any-thing for him. He's a good boy. Deserves a break. It's his own damn business how quick he falls for a girl. Why don't you try and give him a hand?

Patman exhaled wearily and turned back into the hut. He lifted De Sana's handgun from the holster on the wall and pushed it into the waist of his pants. From the cupboard he took the boxes of cartridges, loading one arm, and then picked up a Winchester leaning in the front corner that he had not noticed there before. He passed around the cooking lean-to to the back of the hut and entered the pines that pushed in close there. In a few minutes he was back inside the cabin, brushing sand from his hands. Not much, he thought, but maybe it'll help some. Before he sat down and poured himself a drink, he drew his pistol and placed it on the table near his hand.

★

Chapter Three

Two Cents knew patience. It was as natural to him as breathing. He could not help smiling as he watched the white man, not a hundred feet away and just above him on the opposite slope, pull his head up high over the rim of the rocks in front of him, concentrating his attention off below where the trail broke into the pass. Rondo watched the pass, like De Sana had told him, and if his eyes wandered over the opposite canyon wall, it was only when he dragged them back to his own niche, and then it was only a fleeting glance at almost vertical smooth rock and brush.

Two Cents waited and watched, studying this white man who exposed himself so in hiding. Perhaps the man is a lure, he thought, to take us off guard. His lips straightened into a tight line, erasing the smile. He watched the man's head turn to the trees above him. Then the head turned back and he lifted the big canteen to his mouth. Two Cents had counted, and it was the sixth time the man had done so in less than a half hour. His thirst must be that of fire.

He felt a hand on his ankle and began to ease his body away from the rim that was here thick with tangled brush. He backed away cautiously so that the loose gravel would not even know he was there, and nodded his head once to Vea Oiga who crept past him to where he had lain.

A dozen or so yards back, where the ground sloped from the rim, he stood erect and looked back at Vea Oiga. Even at this short distance he could barely make out the crouched figure.

He lifted the shell belt over his head and then removed the faded blue jacket carefully, smoothing the bare sleeves before folding it next to Vea Oiga's on the ground. If he performed bravely, he thought, perhaps Cima Quaine will put a gold mark on the sleeves. He noticed Vea Oiga had folded his jacket so the three gold stripes were on top. Perhaps not three all at once, for it had taken Vea Oiga years to acquire them, but just one. How fine that would look. Surely Cima Quaine must recognize their ability in discovering this man in the pass.

Less than an hour before they had followed the trail up to the point where it twisted into the pass, but there they stopped and back-trailed to a gradual rock fall that led up to the top of the canyon. They had tied up there and climbed on foot to the canyon rim that looked across to the other slope. They had done this naturally, without a second thought, because it was their business, and because if they were laying an ambush they would have picked this place where the pass narrowed and it was a hundred feet back to shelter. A few minutes after creeping to the rim, Rondo had appeared with a clatter of gravel, standing, exposing himself fully.

Vea Oiga had whispered to him what they would do after studying the white man for some time. Then he had dropped back to prepare himself. With Cima Quaine and the rest of the Coyotero Apache scouts less than an hour behind, they would just have time to get ready and go about the ticklish job of disposing of the lookout. Two Cents hoped that the chief scout would hurry up and be there to see him climb up to take the guard. He glanced at his castoff cavalry jacket again and pictured the gold chevron on the sleeve; it was as bright and impressive as Vea Oiga's sergeant stripes.

Now he looked at the curled toes of his moccasins as he unfastened the ties below his knees and rolled the legging part of his pants high above his knees and secured them again. He tightened the string of his breechclout, then spit on his hands a half dozen times rubbing the saliva over his arms and the upper part of his body until his dull brown coloring glistened with the wetness. When he had moistened every part of skin showing, he sank to the ground and rolled in the dust, rubbing his arms and face with the sand that clung to the wet skin.

He raised himself to his knees and knelt motionless like a rock or a stump, his body the color of everything around him, and now, just as still and unreal in his concentration.

Slowly his arms lifted to the dulling sky and his thoughts went to U-sen. He petitioned the God that he might perform bravely in what was to come, and if it were the will of U-sen that he was to die this day, would the God mind if it came about before the sun set? To be killed at night was to wander in eternal darkness, and nothing that he imagined could be worse, especially coming at the hands of a white man whom even the other white men despised.

* * *

WHEN TWO CENTS had disappeared down through the rocks, Vea Oiga moved back from the rim until he was sure he could not be seen. Then he ran in a crouch, weaving through the mesquite and boulders, until he found another place along the rim that was dense with brush clumps. From here, Rondo's head and rifle barrel were still visible, but now he could also see, down to the right, the opening where the trail cut into the pass. He lay motionless watching the white man until finally the low, wailing call lifted from down-canyon. At that moment he watched Rondo more intently and saw the man's head lift suddenly to look in the direction from which the sound had come; but after only a few seconds the head dropped again, relaxed. Vea Oiga smiled. Now it was his turn.

The figure across the canyon was still for a longer time than usual, but finally the scout saw the head move slowly, looking behind and above to the pines. Vea Oiga rolled to his side and cupped his hands over his mouth. When he saw the canteen come up even with the man's face, he whistled into his cupped hands, the sound coming out in a moan and floating in the air as if coming from nowhere. He rolled again in time to see Two Cents dart from the trail opening across the pass to the opposite slope. He lay motionless at the base for a few minutes. Then as he watched, the figure slowly began to inch his way up-canyon.

By the time the sergeant of scouts had made his way around to where trail met pass, Two Cents was far up the canyon. Vea Oiga clung tight to the rock wall and inched his face past the angle that would show him the pass. He saw the movement. A hump that was part of the ground seemed to edge along a few feet and then stop. And soon he watched this moving piece of earth glide directly under the white man's position and dissolve into the hollow that ran up the slanting wall just past the yellowness of the patch of prickly pear. And above the yellow bloom the rifle could no longer be seen. A splash of crimson spreading in the sky behind the pines was all that was left of the sun.

Vea Oiga turned quickly and ran back up-trail. He stopped on a rise and looked out over the open country, patched and cut with hills in the distance. His gaze crawled out slowly, sweeping on a small arc, and then stopped. There! Yes, he was sure. Maybe they were three miles away, but no more, which meant Cima Quaine would be there in fif-

teen to twenty minutes. Vea Oiga did not have time
to wait for the scouting party. He ran back to the
mouth of the pass and there, at the side of the trail,
piled three stones one on the other. With his knife
he scratched marks on the top stone and at the base
of the bottom one, then hurried to the outcropping
of rock from which he had watched the progress of
his companion. And just as his gaze inched past the
rock, he saw the movement behind and above the
white man's position, as if part of the ground was
sliding down on him.

Vea Oiga moved like a shadow at that moment
across the openness of the pass. The shadow moved
quickly up the face of the slope and soon was lost
among rock and the darkness of the pines that
straggled down the slope.

★ ★ ★

CROSSING THE CLEAR patch of sand, Lew De Sana
didn't like the feeling that had come over him. Not
something new, just an intensifying of the nervousness that had spread through his body since the arrival of the two men. As if every part of his body
was aware of something imminent, but would not
tell his mind about it. As he thought about it, he realized that, no, it was not something that had been
born with the arrival of the two men. It had been

inside of him every day of the two years at Yuma, gaining strength the night Rondo aided him in his escape. And it had been a clawing part of his stomach the night north of Tucson when they had picked up the girl.

He didn't understand the feeling. That's what worried him. The nervousness would come and then go away, but when it returned, he would find that it had grown, and when it went away there was always a part of him that had vanished with it. A part of him that he used to rely on.

One thing, he was honest with himself in his introspection. And undoubtedly it was this honesty that made him see himself clearly enough to be frightened, but still with a certain haze that would not allow him to understand. He remembered his reputation. Cold nerve and a swivel-type gun holster that he knew how to use. In the days before Yuma, sometimes reputation had been enough. And, more often, he had hoped that it would be enough, for he wasn't fool enough to believe completely in his own reputation. But every once in a while he was called on to back up his reputation, and sometimes this had been hard.

Now he wasn't sure. Men can forget in two years. They can forget a great deal, and De Sana worried if he would have to prove himself all over again. It had come to him lately that if this were true, he would never survive, even though he knew he was still good with a gun and could face any situation if he had to. There was this tiredness inside of him now. It clashed with the nervous tension of a hunted man and left him confused and in a desperate sort of helplessness.

Moving through the pines, thoughts ran through his mind, one on top of the other so that none of them made sense. He closed his eyes tightly for a moment, passing his hand over his face and rubbing his forehead as if the gesture would make the racing in his mind stop. He felt the short hair hanging on his forehead, and as his hand lowered, the gauntness of his cheeks and the stubble of his new mustache. He saw the cell block at Yuma and swore in his breath.

His boots made a muffled, scraping sound moving over the sand and pine needles, and, as if becoming aware of the sound for the first time, he slowed his steps and picked his way more carefully through the trees.

The muscles in his legs tightened as he eased his steps on the loose ground. And then he stopped. He stopped dead and the pistol was out in front of him before he realized he had even pulled it. Instinctively his knees bent slightly as he crouched; straining his neck forward he looked through the dimness of the pines, but if there was movement before, it was not there now.

Still, he waited a few minutes to make sure. He let the breath move through his lips in a long sigh and lowered the pistol to his side. He hated himself for his jumpiness. It was the strange tiredness again. He was tired of hiding and drawing when the wind moved the branches of trees. How much can a man take, he wondered. Maybe staying alive wasn't worth it when you had to live this way.

* * *

HE WAS ABOUT to go ahead when he saw it again. The pistol came up and this time he was sure. Through the branches of the tree in front of him, he saw the movement, a shadow gliding from one clump to the next, perhaps fifty paces up ahead. Now, as he crouched low to the bole of the pine that shielded him, the lines in his face eased. At that moment he felt good because it wasn't jumpiness anymore, and there was another feeling within him that hadn't been there for a long time. He peered through the thick lower branches of the pine and saw the dim shape on the path now moving directly toward him.

He watched the figure stop every few feet, still shadowy in the gloom, then move ahead a little more before stopping to look right and left and even behind. De Sana felt the tightness again in his stomach, not being able to make out what the man was, and suddenly the panic was back. For a split second he imagined one of the shadows that had been haunting him had suddenly become a living thing; and then he made out the half-naked Apache and it was too late to imagine anymore.

He knew there would be a noise when he made his move, but that couldn't be helped. He waited until the Indian was a step past the tree, then he raised up. Coal-black hair flaired suddenly from a shoulder, then a wide-eyed face even with his own and an open mouth that almost cried out before the pistol barrel smashed against the bridge of his nose and forehead.

De Sana cocked his head, straining against the silence, then slowly eased down next to the body of the Indian when no sound reached him. He thought: A body lying motionless always seemed to make it more quiet. Like the deeper silence that seemed to follow gunfire. Probably the silence was just in your head.

He laid his hand on the thin, grimy chest and jerked it back quickly when he felt no movement. Death wasn't something the outlaw was squeamish about, but it surprised him that the blow to the head had killed the Indian. He looked over the half-

naked figure calmly and decided there was something there that bothered him. He bent closer in the
gloom. No war paint. Not a line. He fumbled at the
Indian's holster hurriedly and pulled out the well-
kept Colt .44. No reservation-jumping buck owned
a gun like that; and even less likely, a Sierra Madre
broncho who'd more probably carry a rusted cap
and ball at best. He wondered why it hadn't occurred to him right away. Apache police! And that
meant Cima Quaine. . . .

He stood up and listened again momentarily before moving ahead quickly through the pines.

He came to the canyon rim and edged along it
cautiously, pressing close to the flinty rock, keeping
to the deep shadows as much as he could, until he
reached the hollow that sloped to the niche that
Rondo had dug for himself.

He jumped quickly into the depression that fell
away below him and held himself motionless in the
darkness of the hollow for almost a minute before
edging his gaze over the side and down to the niche a
dozen yards below. He saw Rondo sprawled on his
back with one booted leg propped on the rock para-
pet next to the rifle that pointed out over the pass.

There was no hesitating now. He climbed hurriedly, almost frantically, back to the pine grove
and ran against the branches that stung his face and

made him stumble in his haste. The silence was still there, but now it was heavier, pushing against him to make him run faster and stumble more often in the loose footing of the sand. He didn't care if he made noise. He heard his own forced breathing close and loud and imagined it echoing over the hillside, but now he didn't care because they knew he was here. He knew he was afraid. Things he couldn't see did that to him. He reached the clearing, finally, and darted across the clearing toward the hut.

★

Chapter Four

Virgil Patman pushed the glass away from his hand when he heard the noise outside and wrapped his fingers around the bone handle of the pistol. The light slanting through the open doorway was weak, almost the last of the sun. He waited for the squat figure of Rondo to appear in this dim square of light, and started slightly when suddenly a thin shape appeared. And he sat bolt upright when next De Sana was in the room, clutching the door frame and breathing hard.

Patman watched him curiously and managed to

keep the surprise out of his voice when he asked, "Where's Rondo? Thought you relieved him."

De Sana gasped out the word, "Quaine!" and wheeled to the front corner where the rifle had been. He took two steps and stopped dead. Patman watched the thin shoulders stiffen and raised the pistol with his hand still on the table until the barrel was leveled at the outlaw.

"So you led them here after all." His voice was low, almost a mumble, but the hate in the words cut against the stillness of the small room. He looked directly into Patman's face, as if not noticing the pistol leveled at him. "I must be getting old," he said in the same quiet tone.

"You're not going to get a hell of a lot older," Patman answered. "But I'll tell you this. We didn't bring Quaine and his Apaches here. You can believe that or not. I don't much care. Just all of a sudden I don't think you're doing anybody much good being alive."

De Sana's mouth eased slightly as he smiled. "Why don't you let your boy do his own fighting?" And with the words he looked calmed again, as if he didn't care that a trap was tightening about him. Patman noticed it, because he had seen the panic on his face when he entered. Now he saw this calm returning and wondered if it was just a last-act bravado. It unnerved him a little to see a man so at ease with a gun turned on him and he lifted the pistol a foot off the table to make sure the outlaw had seen it.

"I'm not blind."

"Just making sure, Lew," Patman drawled.

De Sana seemed to relax even more now, and moved his hand to his back pocket, slowly, so the other man wouldn't get the wrong idea. He said, "Mind if I have a smoke?" while he dug the tobacco and paper from his pocket.

Patman shook his head once from side to side, and his eyes squinted at the outlaw, wondering what the hell he was playing for. He looked closely as the man poured tobacco into the creased paper and didn't see any of it shake loose to the floor. The fool's got iron running through him, he thought.

De Sana looked up as he shaped the cigarette. "You didn't answer my question," he said.

"About the boy? He can take care of himself," Patman answered.

"Why isn't he here, then?" De Sana said it in a low voice, but there was a sting to the words.

Patman said, "He's out courting your girlfriend," and smiled, watching the dumbfounded expression freeze on the gunman's face. "You might say I'm giving him a little fatherly hand here," and the smile broadened.

De Sana's thin body had stiffened. Now he breathed long and shrugged his shoulders. "So you're playing the father," he said. Standing half-sideways toward Patman, he pulled the unlit cigarette from his mouth and waved it at the man seated behind the table. "I got to reach for a match, Dad."

"Long as you can do it with your left hand," Patman said. Then added, "Son."

De Sana smiled thinly and drew a match from his side pocket.

Patman watched the arm swing down against the thigh and saw the sudden flame in the dimness as it came back up. And at that split second he knew he had made his mistake.

He saw the other movement, another something swinging up, but it was off away from the sudden flare of the match and in the fraction of the moment it took him to realize what it was, it was too late. There was the explosion, the stab of flame, and the shock against his arm. At the same time he went up from the table and felt the weight of the handgun slipping from his fingers, as another explosion mixed with the smoke of the first and he felt the sledgehammer blow against his side. He went over with the chair and felt the packed-dirt floor slam against his back.

His hands clutched at his side instinctively, feeling the wetness that was there already, then winced in pain and dropped his right arm next to him on the floor. He closed his eyes hard, and when he opened them again he was looking at a pistol barrel, and above it De Sana's drawn face.

Unsmiling, the outlaw said, "I don't think you'd a made a very good father." He turned quickly and sprinted out of the hut.

Patman closed his eyes again to see the swirling black that sucked at his brain. For a moment he felt a nausea in his stomach, then numbness seemed to creep over his body. A prickling numbness that was as soothing as the dark void that was spinning inside his head. *I'm going to sleep,* he thought. But before he did, he remembered hearing a shot come from outside, then another.

★ ★ ★

CIMA QUAINE WALKED over to him when he saw the boy look up quickly.

Dave Fallis looked anxiously from Patman's motionless form up to the chief scout who now stood next to him where he knelt.

"I saw his eyes open and close twice!" he whispered excitedly.

The scout hunkered down beside him and wrinkled his buckskin face into a smile. It was an ageless face, cold in its dark, crooked lines and almost cruel, but the smile was plain in the eyes. He was bare-headed, and his dark hair glistened flat on his skull in the lantern light that flickered close behind him on the table.

"You'd have to tie rocks to him and drop him in a well to kill Virgil," he said. "And then you'd never be sure." He glanced at the boy to see the effect of his words and then back to Patman. The eyes were open now, and Patman was grinning at him.

"Don't be too sure," he said weakly. His eyes went to Fallis who looked as if he wanted to say something, but was afraid to let it come out. He smiled back at the boy watching the relief spread over his face and saw him bite at his lower lip. "Did you get him?"

Fallis shook his head, but Quaine said, "Vea Oiga was crawling up to take the horses when De Sana ran into the corral and took one without even waiting to saddle. He shot at him, but didn't get him." He twisted his head and looked up at one of the Apaches standing behind him. "When we get home, you're going to spend your next two months' pay on practice shells."

Vea Oiga dropped his head and looked suddenly ashamed and ridiculous with the vermilion sergeant stripes painted on his naked arms. He shuffled through the doorway without looking up at the girl who stepped inside quickly to let him pass.

She stood near the cupboard not knowing what to do with her hands, watching Dave Fallis. One of the half-dozen Coyotero scouts in the room moved near her idly, and she shrank closer to the wall nervously picking at the frayed collar of her dress. She looked about the room wide-eyed for a moment, then stepped around the Apache hurriedly and out through the doorway. She moved toward the lean-to, but held up when she saw the three Apaches inside laughing and picking at the strips of venison that were hanging from the roof to dry. After a while, Fallis got up stretching the stiffness from his legs and walked to the door. He stood there looking out, but seeing just the darkness.

Cima Quaine bent closer to Patman's drawn face. The ex-trooper's eyes were open, but his face was tight with pain. The hole in his side had started to bleed again. Patman knew it was only a matter of time, but he tried not to show the pain when the

contract scout lowered close to him. He heard the
scout say, "Your partner's kind of nervous," and for
a moment it sounded far away.

Patman answered, "He's young," but knew that
didn't explain anything to the other man.

"He's anxious to get on after the man," Quaine
went on. "How you feel having an avenging angel?" Then added quickly, "Hell, in another day or
two you'll be avenging yourself."

"It's not for me," Patman whispered, and hesitated. "It's for himself, and the girl."

Quaine was surprised, but kept his voice down.
"The girl? He hasn't even looked at her since we
got here."

"And he won't," Patman said. "Until he gets
him." He saw the other man's frown and added,
"It's a long story, all about pride and getting your
toes stepped on." He grinned to himself at the faint
sign of bewilderment on the scout's face. Nobody's
going to ask a dying man to talk sense. Besides, it
would take too long.

After a silence, Patman whispered, "Let him go,
Cima."

"His yen to make war might be good as gold, but
my boys ain't worth a damn after dark. We can
pick up the man's sign in the morning and have him
before sundown."

"You do what you want tomorrow. Just let him go tonight."

"He wouldn't gain anything," the scout whispered impatiently. "He's got the girl here now to live with long as he wants."

"He's got to live with himself, too." Patman's voice sounded weaker. "And he doesn't take free gifts. He's got a funny kind of pride. If he doesn't go after that man, he'll never look at that girl again."

Cima Quaine finished, "And if he does go after him, he may not get the chance. No, Virg. I better keep him here. He can come along tomorrow if he wants." He turned his head as if that was the end of the argument and looked past the Coyoteros to see the girl standing in the doorway.

She came in hesitantly, dazed about the eyes, as if a strain was sapping at her vitality to make her appear utterly spent. She said, "He's gone," in a voice that was not her own.

Cima Quaine's head swung back to Patman when he heard him say, "Looks like you don't have anything to say about it."

✴ ✴ ✴

AT THE FIRST light of dawn, Dave Fallis looked out over the meadow from the edge of timber and was unsure. There was moisture in the air lending a thickness to the gray dawn, but making the boundless stillness seem more empty. Mist will do that, for it isn't something in itself. It goes with lonesomeness and sometimes has a feeling of death. He reined his horse down the slight grade and crossed the gray wave of meadow, angling toward the dim outline of a draw that trailed up the ridge there. It cut deep into the tumbled rock, climbing slowly. After a while he found himself on a bench and stopped briefly to let his horse rest for a moment. The mist was below him now, clinging thickly to the meadow and following it as it narrowed through the valley ahead. He continued on along the bench that finally ended, forcing him to climb on into switchbacks that shelved the steepness of the ridge. And after two hours of following the ridge crown, he looked down to estimate himself a good eight miles ahead of the main trail that stayed with the meadow. He went down the opposite slope, not so steep here, but still following switchbacks, until he was in level country again and heading for the Escudillas in the distance.

The sun made him hurry. For every hour it climbed in the sky lessened his chance of catching the man before the Coyoteros did. He was going on luck. The Coyoteros would use method. But now he wondered if it was so much luck. Vea Oiga had told him what to do.

He had been leading the horse out of the corral and down through the timber when Vea Oiga grew out of the shadows next to him, also leading a horse. The Indian handed the reins to the boy and held back the mare he had been leading. "It is best you take gelding," he whispered. "The man took stallion. Leave the mare here so there is no chance she will call to her lover."

The Apache stood close to him confidently. "You have one chance, man," he said. "Go to Bebida Wells, straight, without following the trail. The man will go fast for a time, until he learns he is not being followed. But at dawn he will go quick again on the main trail for that way he thinks he will save time. But soon he will tire and will need water. Then he will go to Bebida Wells, for that is the only water within one day of here. When he reaches the well, he will find his horse spent and his legs weary from hanging without stirrups. And there he will rest until he can go on."

He had listened, fascinated, while the Indian read into the future and then heard how he should angle, following the draws and washes to save miles. For a moment he wondered about this Indian who knew him so well in barely more than an hour, how he had anticipated his intent, why he was helping. It had made no sense, but it was a course to follow, something he had not had before. The Apache had told him, "Shoot straight, man. Shoot before he sees you."

And with the boy passing from view into the darkness, Vea Oiga led the mare back to the corral, thinking of the boy and the dying man in the hut. Revenge was something he knew, but it never occurred to him that a woman could be involved. And if the boy failed, then he would get another chance to shoot straight. There was always plenty of time.

★ ★ ★

THE SUN WAS almost straight up, crowding the whole sky with its brassy white light, when he began climbing again. The Escudillas seemed no closer, but now the country had turned wild, and from a rise he could see the wildness tangling and growing into gigantic rock formations as it reached and climbed toward the sawtooth heights of the Escudillas.

He had been angling to come around above the wells, and now, in the heights again, he studied the ravines and draws below him and judged he had overshot by only a mile. On extended patrols out of

Thomas they had often hit for Bebida before making the swing-back to the south. It was open country approaching the wells, so he had skirted wide to come in under cover of the wildness and slightly from behind.

A quarter of a mile on he found a narrow draw dense with pines strung out along the walls, the pines growing into each other and bending across to form a tangled arch over the draw. He angled down into its shade and picketed the gelding about halfway in. Then, lifting the Winchester, he passed out of the other end and began threading his way across the rocks.

A yard-wide defile opened up on a ledge that skirted close to the smoothness of boulders, making him edge sideways along the shadows of the towering rocks, until finally the ledge broadened and fell into a ravine that was dense with growth, dotted with pale yucca stalks against the dark green. He ran through the low vegetation in a crouch and stopped to rest at the end of the ravine where once more the ground turned to grotesque rock formations. Not a hundred yards off to the left, down through an opening in the rocks, he made out the still, sand-colored water of a well.

More cautiously now, he edged through the rocks, moving his boots carefully on the flinty

ground. And after a dozen yards of this he crept
into the narrowness of two boulders that hung
close together, pointing the barrel of the Winchester through the aperture toward the pool of muddy
water below.

He watched the vicinity of the pool with a grim-
ness now added to his determination; he watched
without reflecting on why he was there. He had
thought of that all morning: seeing Virg die on the
dirt floor. . . . But the outlaw's words had always
come up to blot that scene. "I think you better
teach him the facts of life." Stepping on his toes
while he was supposed to smile back. It embarrassed him because he wanted to be here because of
Virg. First Virg and then the girl. He told himself
he was doing this because Virg was his friend, and
because the girl was helpless and couldn't defend
herself and deserved a chance. That's what he told
himself.

But that was all in the past, hazy pictures in his
mind overshadowed by the business at hand. He
knew what he was doing there, if he wasn't sure
why. So that when the outlaw's thin shape came
into view below him, he was not excited.

He did not see where De Sana had come from,
but realized now that he must have been hiding
somewhere off to the left. De Sana crouched low

behind a scramble of rock and poked his carbine below toward the pool, looking around as if trying to determine if this was the best position overlooking the well. His head turned, and he looked directly at the aperture behind him, where the two boulders met, studying it for a long moment before turning back to look down his carbine barrel at the pool. Dave Fallis levered the barrel of the Winchester down a fraction and the front sight was dead center on De Sana's back.

He wondered why De Sana had taken a carbine from the corral lean-to and not a saddle. Then he thought of Vea Oiga who had fired at him as he fled. And this brought Vea Oiga's words to memory. "Shoot before he sees you."

Past the length of the oiled gun barrel, he saw the Y formed by the suspenders and the faded underwear top, darkened with perspiration. The short-haired skull, thin and hatless. And at the other end, booted long legs, and toes that kicked idly at the gravel.

For a moment he felt sorry for De Sana. Not because the barrel in front of him was trained on his back. He watched the man gaze out over a vastness that would never grow smaller. Straining his eyes for a relentless something that would sooner or later hound him to the ground. And he was all alone. He watched him kick his toes for something to do and wipe the sweat from his forehead with the back of his hand. De Sana perspired like everyone else. That's why he felt sorry for him. He saw a man, like a thousand others he had seen, and he wondered how you killed a man.

The Indian had told him, "Shoot before he sees you." Well, that was just like an Indian.

He moved around from behind the rocks and stood there in plain view with the rifle still pointed below. He felt naked all of a sudden, but brought the rifle up a little and called, "Throw your gun down and turn around!"

And the next second he was firing. He threw the lever and fired again—then a third time. He sat down and ran his hand over the wetness on his forehead, looking at the man who was now sprawled on his back with his carbine across his chest.

He buried the gunman well away from the pool and scattered rocks around so that when he was finished you'd wouldn't know that a grave was there. He took the outlaw's horse and his guns. That would be enough proof. On the way back he kept thinking of Virg and the girl. He hoped that Virg would still be alive, but knew that was too much to ask. Virg and he had had their good times and that was that. That's how you had to look at things.

He thought of the girl and wondered if she'd think he was rushing things if he asked her to go with him to the Panhandle, after a legal ceremony. . . .

And all the way back, not once did he think of Lew De Sana.

2

The Hard Way

TIO ROBLES STRETCHED stiffly on the straw mattress, holding the empty mescal bottle upright on his chest. His sleepy eyes studied Jimmy Robles going through his ritual. Tio was half smiling, watching with amusement.

Jimmy Robles buttoned his shirt carefully, even the top button, and pushed the shirttail tightly into his pants, smooth and tight with no blousing about the waist. It made him move stiffly the few minutes he was conscious of keeping the clean shirt smooth and unwrinkled. He lifted the gun belt from a wall peg and buckled it around his waist, inhaling slowly, watching the faded cotton stretch tight across his stomach. And when he wiped his high black boots it was with the same deliberate care.

Tio's sleepy smile broadened. "Jaime," he spoke softly, "you look very pretty. Are you to be married today?" He waited. "Perhaps this is a feast day that has slipped my mind." He waited longer. "No? Or perhaps the mayor has invited you to dine with him."

Jimmy Robles picked up the sweat-dampened shirt he had taken off and unpinned the silver badge from the pocket. Before looking at his uncle he breathed on the metal and rubbed its smooth surface over the tight cloth of his chest. He pinned it to the clean shirt, studying the inscription cut into the metal that John Benedict had told him read *Deputy Sheriff*.

Sternly, he said, "You drink too much," but could not help smiling at this picture of indolence sprawled on the narrow bed with a foot hooked on the window ledge above, not caring particularly if the world ended at that moment.

"Why don't you stop for a few days, just to see what it's like?"

Tio closed his eyes. "The shock would kill me."

"You're killing yourself anyway."

Tio mumbled, "But what a fine way to die."

Jimmy left the adobe hut and crossed a backyard before passing through the narrow dimness of two adobes that squeezed close together, and when he reached the street he tilted his hat closer to his eyes against the afternoon glare and walked up the street toward Arivaca's business section. This was a part of Saturday afternoon. This leaving the Mexican section that was still quiet, almost deserted, and walking up the almost indiscernible slope that led to the more prosperous business section.

Squat gray adobe grew with the slope from Spanishtown into painted, two-story false fronts with signs hanging from the ramadas. Soon, cowmen from the nearer ranges and townspeople who had quit early because it was Saturday would be standing around under the ramadas, slapping each other on the shoulder thinking about Saturday night. Those who hadn't started already. And Jimmy Robles would smile at everybody and be friendly because he liked this day better than any other. People were easier to get along with. Even the Americans.

Being deputy sheriff of Arivaca wasn't a hard job, but Jimmy Robles was new. And his newness made him unsure. Not confident of his ability to uphold the law and see that the goods and rights of these people were protected while they got drunk on Saturday night.

The sheriff, John Benedict, had appointed him a month before because he thought it would be good for the Mexican population. One of their own boys. John Benedict said you performed your duty "in the name of the law." That was the thing to remember. And it made him feel uneasy because the law was such a big thing. And justice. He wished he could picture something other than that woman with the blindfold over her eyes. John Benedict spoke long of these things. He was a great man.

Not only had he made him deputy, but John Benedict had given him a pair of American boots and a pistol, free, which had belonged to a man who had been hanged the month before. Tio Robles had told him to destroy the hanged man's goods, for it was a bad sign; but that's all Tio knew about it. He was too much *Mexicano*. He would go on sweating at the wagonyard, grumbling, and drinking more mescal than he could hold. It was good he lived with Tio and was able to keep him out of trouble. Not all, some.

His head was down against the glare and he watched his booted feet move over the street dust, lost in thought. But the gunfire from up-street brought him to instantly. He broke into a slow trot, seeing a lone man in the street a block ahead. As he approached him, he angled toward the boardwalk lining the buildings.

★ ★ ★

SID ROMAN STOOD square in the middle of the street with his feet planted wide. There was a stubble of beard over the angular lines of his lower face and his eyes blinked sleepily. He jabbed another cartridge at the open cylinder of the Colt, and fumbled trying to insert it into one of the small openings. The nose of the bullet missed the groove and slipped from his fingers. Sid Roman was drunk, which wasn't unusual, though it wasn't evident from his face. The glazed expression was natural.

Behind him, two men with their hats tilted loosely over their eyes sat on the steps of the Samas Café, their boots stretched out into the street. A half-full bottle was between them on the ramada step. A third man lounged on his elbows against the hitch rack, leaning heavily like a dead weight. Jimmy Robles moved off the boardwalk and stood next to the man on the hitch rack.

Sid Roman loaded the pistol and waved it carelessly over his head. He tried to look around at the men behind him without moving his feet and stumbled off balance, almost going down.

"Come on . . . who's got the money!" His eyes, heavy lidded, went to the two men on the steps. "Hey, Walt, dammit! Put up your dollar!"

The one called Walt said, "I got it. Go ahead and shoot," and hauled the bottle up to his mouth.

Sid Roman yelled to the man on the hitch rack, "You in, Red?" The man looked up, startled, and stared around as if he didn't know where he was.

Roman waved his pistol toward the high front of the saloon across the street. SUPREME, in foot-high red letters, ran across the board hanging from the top of the ramada. "A dollar I put five straight in the top loop of the *P*." He slurred his words impatiently.

Jimmy Robles heard the man next to him mumble, "Sure, Sid." He looked at the sign, squinting hard, but could not make out any bullet scars near the *P*. Maybe there was one just off to the left of the *S*. He waited until the cowman turned and started to raise the Colt.

"Hey, Sid." Jimmy Robles smiled at him like a friend. "I got some good targets out back of the jail."

Aiming, Sid Roman turned irritably, hot in the face. Then the expression was blank and glassy again.

"How'd you know my name?"

Jimmy Robles smiled, embarrassed. "I just heard this man call you that."

Roman looked at him a long time. "Well you heard wrong," he finally said. "It's Mr. Roman."

A knot tightened the deputy's mouth, but he kept the smile on his lips even though its meaning was gone. "All right, mester. It's all the same to me." John Benedict said you had to be courteous.

The man was staring at him hard, weaving slightly. He had heard of Sid Roman, old man Remillard's top hand, but this was the first time he had seen him close. He stared back at the beard-grubby face and felt uneasy because the face was so expressionless—looking him over like he was a dead tree stump. Why couldn't he get laughing drunk like the Mexican boys, then he could be laughing, too, when he took his gun away from him.

"Why don't you just keep your mouth shut," Roman said, as if that was the end of it. But then he added, "Go on and sweep out your jailhouse," grinning and looking over at the men on the steps.

The one called Walt laughed out and jabbed at the other man with his elbow.

Jimmy Robles held on to the smile, gripping it with only his will now. He said, "I'm just thinking of the people. If a stray shot went inside, somebody might get hurt."

"You saying I can't shoot, or're you just chicken scared!"

"I'm just saying there are many people on the street and inside there."

"You're talking awful damn big for a dumb Mex kid. You must be awful dumb." He looked toward the steps, handling the pistol idly. "He must be awful dumb, huh, Walt?"

Jimmy Robles heard the one called Walt mumble, "He sure must," but he kept his eyes on Roman, who walked up to him slowly, still looking at him like he was a stump or something that couldn't talk back or hear. Now, only a few feet away, he saw a glimmer in the sleepy eyes as if a new thought was punching its way through his head.

"Maybe we ought to learn him something, Walt. Seeing he's so dumb." Grinning now, he looked straight into the Mexican boy's eyes. "Maybe I ought to shoot his ears off and give 'em to him for a present. What you think of that, Walt?"

Jimmy Robles's smile had almost disappeared. "I think I had better ask you for your gun, mester." His voice coldly polite.

Roman's stubble jaw hung open. It clamped shut

and his face colored, through the weathered tan it colored as if it would burst open from ripeness. He mumbled through his teeth, "You two-bit kid!" and tried to bring the Colt up.

Robles swung his left hand wide as hard as he could and felt the numbing pain up to his elbow the same time Sid Roman's head snapped back. He tried to think of courtesy, his pistol, the law, the other three men, but it wasn't any of these that drew his hand back again and threw the fist hard against the face that was falling slowly toward him. The head snapped back and the body followed it this time, heels dragging in the dust off balance until Roman was spread-eagled in the street, not moving. He swung on the three men, pulling his pistol.

They just looked at him. The one called Walt shrugged his shoulders and lifted the bottle that was almost empty.

★　★　★

WHEN JOHN BENEDICT closed the office door behind him, his deputy was coming up the hall that connected the cells in the rear of the jail. He sat down at the rolltop desk, hearing the footsteps in the bare hallway, and swiveled his chair, swinging his back to the desk.

"I was over to the barbershop. I saw you bring

somebody in," he said to Jimmy Robles entering the office. "I was all lathered up and couldn't get out. Saw you pass across the street, but couldn't make out who you had."

Jimmy Robles smiled. "Mester Roman. Didn't you hear the shooting?"

"Sid Roman?" Benedict kept most of the surprise out of his voice. "What's the charge?"

"He was drinking out in the street and betting on shooting at the sign over the Supreme. There were a lot of people around—" He wanted to add, "John," because they were good friends, but Benedict was old enough to be his father and that made a difference.

"So then he called you something and you got mad and hauled him in."

"I tried to smile, but he was pointing his gun all around. It was hard."

John Benedict smiled at the boy's serious face. "Sid call you chicken scared?"

Jimmy Robles stared at this amazing man he worked for.

"He calls everybody that when he's drunk." Benedict smiled. "He's a lot of mouth, with nothing coming out. Most times he's harmless, but someday he'll probably shoot somebody." His eyes wandered out the window. Old man Remillard was crossing the street toward the jail. "And then we'll get the blame for not keeping him here when he's full of whiskey."

Jimmy Robles went over the words, his smooth features frowning in question. "What do you mean we'll get blamed?"

Benedict started to answer him, but changed his mind when the door opened. Instead, he said, "Afternoon," nodding his head to the thick, big-boned man in the doorway. Benedict followed the rancher's gaze to Jimmy Robles. "Mr. Remillard, Deputy Sheriff Robles."

Remillard's face was serious. "Quit kidding," he said. He moved toward the sheriff. "I'm just fixing up a mistake you made. Your memory must be backing up on you, John." He was unexcited, but his voice was heavy with authority. Remillard hadn't been told no in twenty years, not by anyone, and his air of command was as natural to him as breathing. He handed Benedict a folded sheet he had pulled from his inside coat pocket, nodding his head toward Jimmy Robles.

"You better tell your boy what end's up."

He waited until Benedict looked up from the sheet of paper, then said, "I was having my dinner with Judge Essery at the Samas when my foreman was arrested. Essery's waived trial and suspended sentence. It's right there, black and white. And kind of lucky for you, John, the judge's in a good mood today." Remillard walked to the door, then turned back. "It isn't in the note, but you better have my boy out in ten minutes." That was all.

John Benedict read the note over again. He remembered the first time one like it was handed to him, five years before. He had read it over five times and had almost torn it up, before his sense returned. He wondered if he was using the right word, *sense*.

"Let him out and give him his gun back."

Jimmy Robles smiled, because he thought the sheriff was kidding. He said, "Sure," and the "John" almost slipped out with it. He propped his hip against the edge of his table-desk.

"What are you waiting for?"

Jimmy Robles came off the table now, and his face hung in surprise. "Are you serious?"

Benedict held out the note. "Read this five times and then let him go."

"But I don't understand," with disbelief all over his face. "This man was endangering lives. You said we were to protect and . . . " His voice trailed off, trying to think of all the things John Benedict had told him.

Sitting in his swivel chair, John Benedict thought, Explain that one if you can. He remembered the words better than the boy did. Now he wondered how he had kept a straight face when he had told him about rights, and the law, and seeing how the one safeguarded the other. That was John Benedict the realist. The cynic. He told himself to shut up. He did believe in ideals. What he had been telling himself for years, though having to close his eyes occasionally because he liked his job.

Now he said to the boy, "Do you like your job?" And Jimmy Robles looked at him as if he did not understand.

He started to tell him how a man elected to a job naturally had a few obligations. And in a town like Arivaca, whose business depended on spreads like Remillard's and a few others, maybe the obligations were a little heavier. It was a cowtown, so the cowman ought to be able to have what he wanted. But it was too long a story to go through. If Jimmy Robles couldn't see the handwriting, let him find out the hard way. He was old enough to figure it out for himself. Suddenly, the boy's open, wondering face made him mad.

"Well, what the hell are you waiting for!"

✯ ✯ ✯

JIMMY ROBLES pushed Tio's empty mescal bottle to the foot of the bed and sat down heavily. He eased back until he was resting on his spine with his head and shoulders against the adobe wall and sat like this for a long time while the thoughts went through his head. He wished Tio were here. Tio would offer no assistance, no explanation other than his biased own, but he would laugh and that would be better than nothing. Tio would say, "What did you expect would happen, you fool?" And add, "Let us have a drink to forget the mysterious ways of the American." Then he would laugh. Jimmy Robles sat and smoked cigarettes and he thought.

Later on, he opened his eyes and felt the ache in his neck and back. It seemed like only a few moments before he had been awake, clouded with his worrying, but the room was filled with a dull gloom. He rose, rubbing the back of his neck, and, through the open doorway that faced west, saw the red streak in the gloom over the line of trees in the distance.

He felt hungry, and the incident of the afternoon was something that might have happened a hundred years ago. He had worn himself out thinking and that was enough of it. He passed between the buildings to the street and crossed it to the adobe with the sign EMILIANO'S. He felt like enchiladas and tacos and perhaps some beer if it was cold.

He ate alone at the counter, away from the crowded tables that squeezed close to each other in the hot, low-ceilinged café, taking his time and listening to the noise of the people eating and drinking. Emiliano served him, and after his meal set another beer—that was very cold—before him on the counter. And when he was again outside, the air seemed cooler and the dusk more restful.

He lighted a cigarette, inhaling deeply, and saw someone emerge from the alley that led to his adobe. The figure looked up and down the street, then ran directly toward him, shouting his name.

Now he recognized Agostino Reyes, who worked at the wagonyard with his uncle.

The old man was breathless. "I have hunted you everywhere," he wheezed, his eyes wide with excitement. "Your uncle has taken the shotgun that they keep at the company office and has gone to shoot a man!"

Robles held him hard by the shoulders. "Speak clearly! Where did he go!"

Agostino gasped out, "Earlier, a man by the Supreme insulted him and caused him to be degraded in front of others. Now Tio has gone to kill him."

Jimmy ran with his heart pounding against his chest, praying to God and His Mother to let him get there before anything happened. A block away from the Supreme he saw the people milling about the street, with all attention toward the front of the saloon. He heard the deep discharge of a shotgun and the people scattered as if the shot were a signal. In the space of a few seconds the street was deserted.

He slowed the motion of his legs and approached the rest of the way at a walk. Nothing moved in front of the Supreme, but across the street he saw figures in the shadowy doorways of the Samas Café and the hotel next door. A man stepped out to the street and he saw it was John Benedict.

"Your uncle just shot Sid Roman. Raked his legs with a Greener. He's up there in the doorway laying half dead."

He made out the shape of a man lying beneath the swing doors of the Supreme. In the dusk the street was quiet, more quiet than he had ever known it, as if he and John Benedict were alone. And then the scream pierced the stillness. "God Almighty somebody help me!" It hung there, a cold wail in the gloom, then died.

"That's Sid," Benedict whispered. "Tio's inside with his pistol. If anybody gets near that door, he'll let go and most likely finish off Sid. He's got Remillard and Judge Essery and I don't know who else inside. They didn't get out in time. God knows what he'll do to them if he gets jumpy."

"Why did Tio shoot him?"

"They say about an hour ago Sid come staggering out drunk and bumped into your uncle and started telling him where to go. But your uncle was just as drunk and he wouldn't take any of it. They started swinging and Sid got Tio down and rubbed his face in the dust, then had one of his boys get a bottle, and he sat there drinking like he was on the front porch. Sitting on Tio. Then the old man come back about an hour later and let go at him with the Greener." John Benedict added, "I can't say I blame him."

Jimmy Robles said, "What were you doing while Sid was on the front porch?" and started toward the Supreme, not waiting for an answer.

John Benedict followed him. "Wait a minute," he called, but stopped when he got to the middle of the street.

On the saloon steps he could see Sid Roman plainly in the square of light under the doors, lying on his back with his eyes closed. A moan came from his lips, but it was almost inaudible. No sound came from within the saloon.

He mounted the first step and stood there. "Tio!"

No answer came. He went all the way up on the porch and looked down at Roman. "Tio! I'm taking this man away!"

Without hesitating he grabbed the wounded man beneath the arms and pulled him out of the doorway to the darkened end of the ramada past the windows. Roman screamed as his legs dragged across the boards. Jimmy Robles moved back to the door and the quietness settled again.

He pushed the door in, hard, and let it swing back, catching it as it reached him. Tio was leaning against the bar with bottles and glasses strung out its smooth length behind him. From the porch he could see no one else. Tio looked like a frightened animal cowering in a dead-end ravine, more pathetic in his ragged and dirty cotton clothes. His rope-soled shoes edged a step toward the doorway, with his body moving in a crouch. The pistol was in front of him, his left hand under the other wrist supporting the weight of the heavy Colt and, the deputy noticed now, trying to keep it steady.

Tio waved the barrel at him. "Come in and join your friends, Jaime." His voice quivered to make the bravado meaningless.

Robles moved inside the door of the long barroom and saw Remillard and Judge Essery standing by the table nearest the bar. Two other men stood at the next table. One of them was the bartender, wiping his hands back and forth over his apron.

Robles spoke calmly. "You've done enough, Tio. Hand me the gun."

"Enough?" Tio swung the pistol back to the first table. "I have just started."

"Don't talk crazy. Hand me the gun."

"Do you think I am crazy?"

"Just hand me the gun."

Tio smiled, and by it seemed to calm. "My foolish nephew. Use your head for one minute. What do you suppose would happen to me if I handed you this gun?"

"The law would take its course," Jimmy Robles said. The words sounded meaningless even to him.

"It would take its course to the nearest cottonwood," Tio said. "There are enough fools in the family with you, Jaime." He smiled still, though his voice continued to shake.

"Perhaps this is my mission, Jaime. The reason I was born."

"You make it hard to decide just which one is the fool."

"No. Hear me. God made Tio Robles to his image and likeness that he might someday blow out the brains of Señores Rema-yard and Essery." Tio's laugh echoed in the long room.

Jimmy Robles looked at the two men. Judge Essery was holding on to the table and his thin face was white with fear, glistening with fear. And for all old man Remillard's authority, he couldn't do a thing. An old Mexican, like a thousand he could buy or sell, could stand there and do whatever he desired because he had slipped past the cowman's zone of influence, past fearing for the future.

Tio raised the pistol to the level of his eyes. It was already cocked. "Watch my mission, Jaime. Watch me send two devils to hell!"

He watched fascinated. Two men were going to die. Two men he hardly knew, but he could feel only hate for them. Not like he might hate a man, but with the anger he felt for a principle that went against his reason. Something big, like injustice. It went through his mind that if these two men died, all injustice would vanish. He heard the word in his mind. His own voice saying it. Injustice. Repeating it, until then he heard only a part of the word.

His gun came out and he pulled the trigger in the motion. Nothing was repeating in his mind, now. He looked down at Tio Robles on the floor and knew he was dead before he knelt over him.

He picked up Tio in his arms like a small child and walked out of the Supreme into the evening dusk. John Benedict approached him and he saw people crowding out into the street. He walked past the sheriff and behind him heard Remillard's booming voice. "That was a close one!" and a scattering of laughter. Fainter then, he heard Remillard again. "Your boy learns fast."

He walked toward Spanishtown, not seeing the faces that lined the street, hardly feeling the limp weight in his arms.

The people, the storefronts, the street—all was hazy—as if his thoughts covered his eyes like a blindfold. And as he went on in the darkness he thought he understood now what John Benedict meant by justice.

3

Trouble at Rindo's Station

★

Chapter One

THERE WAS A TIME when Bonito might have fired at the rider far below on the road, and for no other reason than to test his carbine, since the rider was a white man. He had done this many times before—sometimes for a shirt, or a fresh horse, usually for ammunition, though a reason was not necessary. But now there was something on the Mescalero's mind. He held his fire and urged his pony down the piñon slope.

From high up he had recognized Ross Corsen—

the lank figure slouched in the McClellan saddle, head down against the glare, hat low over his eyes. And now, as the Mescalero closed in, Corsen looked up, though he had seen him long before, when Bonito was still high up the slope.

"*Sik-isn*," Bonito said. The word was a hiss between his lips. Strands of hair hung from the shadow of a high-crowned hat, thick, glistening hair accentuating the yellowish cast of his skin and the pock scars that roughened heavy-boned features. A frayed, sweat-stained shirt covered his chest, but his legs were naked, for he wore only a breechclout, and the curled toes of his moccasins hung beneath the pony's belly, ridiculously close to the ground. A carbine was across his lap.

Ross Corsen smiled at the Apache's greeting and studied the broad, ugly face. "Now you call me *brother*," he said in Spanish. "You must want something." He had not seen the Mescalero in almost a year, not since the four-day chase down to the border, and a glimpse of Bonito far off, not running any longer because he was safely in Mexico. Bonito had killed two Coyotero policemen during a tulapai drunk. That had started it. On the run for the border, he killed two more men, plus four horses that didn't belong to him. Now he was back and Corsen studied him, wondering why.

The Apache spoke a slow, guttural Spanish and said, as if in the middle of his thoughts, "We have suffered unfairly from your hand; all of us have"—he used the Apache word *tinneh,* which meant all of the people and in its meaning described the blood tie which bound them together—"and from the other man, the one who directs you. You think only of yourselves."

"And when did you begin thinking of others?" Corsen said.

"Those are my people at Pinaleño," Bonito answered him.

Corsen shrugged. "I won't argue with you. What you do now is no concern of mine. I can't do a thing to you or for you, but maybe suggest you go home and get drunk, which is what you'll probably do anyway."

"And where is our home, Cor-sen?"

"You know as well as I do."

"At San Carlos, where there is little to eat?"

Corsen nodded to the Maynard carbine across the Apache's lap. "Maybe in Mexico. You can't have one of those at San Carlos."

"Yes, in Sonora and Chihuahua where it is a business of profit to take the hair of the Apache, the government paying for our scalps."

Corsen shook his head. "Look, I no longer am in

charge of the Pinaleño Reservation. The government man has discharged me." He thought for words that would explain it clearly to the Apache. "He is the one, Mr. Sellers, who has taken your guns and decided that you live on government beef."

"Some of the government beef," Bonito corrected. "He sells most of it to others for his own profit."

"That is not true of all reservations. You know I treated your people fairly."

"But you are no longer there and soon it will be true of all reservations."

The words were familiar to Corsen. No, not so much the words as the idea: he had argued this very thing with Sellers three days before, straining his patience to explain to the Bureau of Indian Affairs supervisor exactly what an Apache is. What kind of thinking animal he is. How much abuse he will take before all the peace talks in the world will not stop him. And he had lost the argument because, even if reason was not on Sellers's side, authority was. He threw it in Sellers's face, accusing him of selling government rations for his own profit, and Sellers laughed, daring him to prove it—then fired him. He would have quit. You can't go on working for a man like that. He decided that he didn't care anyway.

For that matter it was strange that he should. Ross Corsen knew Apaches because he had fought them. He had been in charge of the Coyotero trackers at Fort Thomas for four years. And after that, for three years—until the day before yesterday—he had been in charge of the Mescalero Subagency at Pinaleño, thirty miles south of Thomas.

He didn't care. The hell with it. That's what he told himself. Still he kept wondering what had brought Bonito back. He thought: Leave him alone. If he came back to help his people, let him work it out his own Apache way. You tried. But instead he asked carefully, "Why would a warrior of Bonito's stature return now to a reservation? They haven't forgotten what you did. If you're caught, they'll hang you."

"Then I would die—which the people are doing now on the reservation, under Bil-Clin who calls himself their chief." Bonito's eyes half closed and he went on. "Let me tell you a story, Cor-sen, which happened long ago. There was a young man of the Mescalero, who was a great hunter and slayer of his enemies. From raids to Mexico he would return to his rancheria with countless ponies and often with women who would then do his bidding. And many of these he gave to his chief out of honor.

"One day he returned from war gravely wounded and his hands empty, but he noticed that still this chief, who was the son of a chief and he the son of one before him, received more spoils than anyone, yet without endangering himself by being present on the raid. Now this grieved the warrior. He would not offend his chief, but he was beginning to think this unjust.

"On a day after his wound had healed, he was walking in a deep canyon with this in his thoughts and as it grew unbearable he cried out to U-sen why should this be, and immediately a spirit appeared before him. Now, this spirit questioned the warrior, asking him how a man became chief, and the warrior answered that it was blood handed from father to son. And the spirit asked him where in the natural order was this found? Did one lobo wolf lead the pack because of his blood? The warrior thought deeply of this and gradually he realized that chieftainship of blood was not just. It was the place of the bravest warrior to lead—not for his own sake, but for the good of all.

"You know what he did, Cor-sen?" Bonito paused then. "He returned to the rancheria and challenged his chief and fought him to the death with his knife. Two others opposed him, and he killed these also. With this the people realized that it was as it should be and the warrior was acclaimed chief of Mescaleros.

"That was the first time, Cor-sen, but it has happened many times since. When one is no longer deserving to be chief, then another opposes him. Sometimes the opposed chief steps aside; often it is settled with a knife."

Corsen was silent. Then he said, "At Pinaleño Bil-Clin is still a strong chief. And he is wise enough not to lead his people in a war he cannot win."

Bonito's heavy face creased into a grim smile. "Is he strong . . . and wise?" Then he said, his tone changing, "Do you go away from here?"

"Perhaps." Corsen looked at the Apache curiously.

"It would be wise," Bonito said, "if you went far from here." He turned his pony then and loped off.

* * *

Ross Corsen followed the road to Rindo's and the Mescalero's parting words hung in his mind like a threat, and for a while the words made him angry. The running of their tribe was no concern of his. Not now. But it implied more than just Bonito opposing Bil-Clin. There was something else. Bonito was a renegade. He was vicious even in the eyes of his own people. Not the type to be followed as a leader unless the people were desperate. Unless he came just at the right time. And it occurred to Corsen: like now, with a man they don't know taking over the agency . . . and with unrest on every reservation in Arizona, I'd like to stay, just to handle Bonito. . . . But again, the hell with it. Working under Sellers wasn't worth it.

He planned to go up to Whipple Barracks and talk to someone about a guide contract. He would leave his horse at Rindo's and catch the stage there, and while he was waiting he'd have a while to be with Katie.

★

Chapter Two

The Hatch & Hodges' Central Mail section had headquarters at Fort McDowell. From there, one route angled northwest to Prescott. The Central Mail swung in an arc southeast. From McDowell the route skirted the Superstitions to Apache Junction, then continued on, changing teams at Florence, White Tanks, Gila Ford, and Rindo's. Thomas was the last stop, the southern terminal.

Rindo's Station had been constructed with the Apaches in mind. An oblong, thick-walled adobe building had an open stable shed at one end. The corral, holding the spare stage teams, connected behind the stable. And circling the station, out fifty-odd yards, was an adobe wall. It was thick, chest high. At the east end of the yard a stand of aspen had been hacked down and only the trunks remained. Beyond the wall the country was flat on three sides—alkali dust and heat waves shimmering over stubbles of desert growth—but to the east the ground rose gradually, barren, pale yellow climbing into deep green where piñon sprouted from the hillside.

Corsen had skirted the base of the hill and now he was in sight of Rindo's. He nudged his mount to a trot.

Someone was in the doorway. Another figure came from the dark line of the shed and moved to the gate which was in the north side of the wall. He could make out the man in the doorway now—Billy Teachout, the station agent. And as the gate swung open there was the Mexican, Delgado, in white peon clothes.

"Hiiiii, man!"

"Señor Delgado, keeper of the horses!"

Corsen reached down and slapped the old Mexican's thin shoulder, then dismounted.

"God of my life, it has been months!"

"Three or four weeks."

"It seems months."

Corsen grinned at the old man, at the tired eyes

that were now stretched open showing thin lines of veins, smiling at the sight of a friend.

Billy Teachout moved a few steps into the yard, thumbs hooked behind his suspender straps. "Ross, get in here out of the sun!"

"Let the keeper of the horses take yours," Delgado said, still smiling. "We will talk together after."

Corsen followed the station agent's broad back into the house and opened his eyes wide to the interior dimness. It was dark after the sun glare. He pushed his hat brim from his eyes and stood looking at the familiar whitewashed walls, the oblong pine table, and Douglas chairs at one end of the room, the squat stove in the middle, and the red-painted pine bar at the other end. Billy Teachout edged his large frame sideways, with an effort, through the narrow bar opening.

"You wouldn't have beer," Corsen said.

"It's about six months to Christmas," Billy answered, and leaned his forearms onto the bar. He was in no hurry. Time meant little, and it showed in his loose, heavy build, in his round, clean-shaven face that he most always kept out of the sun's reach unless it was stage time. He had worked in the Prescott office until Al Rindo's death two years before, then had been transferred here. Al Rindo had died of a heart attack, but Billy Teachout said it was sunstroke and he'd be damned if he'd let it happen to him. He had Katie to think of, his sister's girl who had come to live with him after her folks passed on.

It wasn't a bad life. Five stages a week for him and Katie; Delgado and his wife to take care of. Change horses; keep them curried; feed the passengers. Nothing to it—as long as the Apaches minded.

"You can have yellow mescal or bar whiskey," Billy said.

"One's as bad as the other." Corsen put his elbows on the bar. "Whiskey."

"Kill any bugs you got."

Corsen took a drink and then rolled a cigarette. "Where's Katie?"

"Prettyin'. She saw you two miles away. After Delgado all week, you don't look so bad."

✵ ✵ ✵

CORSEN GRINNED, relaxing the hard line of his jaw. A young face, leathery and immobile until a smile would soften the eyes that were used to sun glare, and ease the set face that talked eye to eye with the Apache and showed nothing. Corsen knew his business. He knew the Apache—his language, often even his thoughts—and the Apache respected him for it. Corsen, the Indian agent. He could make natural-born raiders at least half satisfied with a barren government land tract. The Corsens were few and far between, even in Arizona.

"Billy, I just saw Bonito."

"God—he's returned to the reservation?"

"I don't know—or much care. I'm leaving."

"What?"

"Sellers fired me day before yesterday. He's got somebody else for the job."

"Got somebody else! Those are Mescaleros!"

"I'm through arguing with him. Sellers is reservation supervisor. He can run things how he likes and hire who he likes. I should have quit long ago."

"Who's taking your place?"

"A man named Verbiest."

"Somebody looking for some extra change."

"He might be all right."

Billy Teachout shook his head wearily. To him it was another example of cheap politics, knowing the right people. Agency posts were being handed out to men who cared nothing for the Indians. There was profit to be made by short-rationing their charges and selling the government beef and grain to homesteaders, or back to the Army. Even that had been done.

"Sellers has been trying to get rid of you for a

long time. Finally he made it," Billy Teachout said. He shook his head again. "Your Mescaleros aren't going to take kindly to this."

"Verbiest might know what he's doing," Corsen said. Then, "But if he doesn't, you better keep your windows shut till he hangs a few of them and they calm down again."

"Where you going? I might just close up and go with you."

"What about the stage line?"

"The hell with it. I'm getting too old for this kind of thing."

Corsen smiled. "I'm going up to Whipple to see about a guide contract."

"So if you can't nurse them, you fight them."

"Either one's a living."

"Ross—"

He turned to see Katie standing in the doorway that led to the kitchen. His gaze rested on her face—tanned, freckled, clear-eyed, a face that smiled often, but now held on his earnestly.

"Ross, I heard what you were telling Billy."

"I can't work for that man anymore."

"Can't you find something else around here?"

"There isn't anything."

"Fort Thomas. Why can't you guide out of there?"

Corsen shrugged. "There's a chance, but I'd still

have to go through the department commander's office at Whipple."

"Ross . . ." Her voice was a whisper.

It showed on her face that was not eager now and seemed even pale beneath the sun coloring. The face of a girl, sensitive nose and mouth, but in her clear, blue, serious eyes the awareness of a woman.

Katie was nineteen. She had known Ross Corsen for almost three years, meeting him the day after she had arrived to live with her uncle. And she expected to marry him, even though he never mentioned it. She knew how he felt. Ross didn't have to say a word. It was in the way he looked at her, in the way he had kissed her for the first time only a few weeks ago—a small, soft, lingering, inexperienced kiss. She loved Corsen; very simply she loved him, because he was a man, respected as a man, and because he was a boy at the same time. Perhaps just as she was girl and woman in one.

"Are you coming back?"

"Of course I am."

"What if you're stationed somewhere far away?"

"I'll come and get you," he answered.

Billy Teachout looked at them, from one to the other. "Maybe I've been inside too much." To the girl he said, "Has he behaved himself?"

"Billy," Corsen said, "I was going to ask you.

This is all of a sudden—" Then, to Katie, "I'm taking the stage." He smiled faintly. "If I leave my horse here, I've got to come back."

★ ★ ★

"THE STAGE!" Delgado was in the doorway momentarily. The screen door banged and he was gone.

It came in from the east, a thin sand trail, a shadow leading the dust that rose furiously into a billowing tail.

Delgado was swinging out with the grayed wooden gate. Then the stage, rumbling in an arc toward the opening, and the hoarse-throated voice of Ernie Ball, the driver.

"Delgadooo!"

The little Mexican was in front of the lead horses now, reaching for reins close to the bit rings.

"Delgado, you half-a-man! Hold 'em, *chico*!"

Ernie Ball was off the box, grinning, wiping the back of a gnarled hand over his mouth, smoothing the waxed tips of his full mustache. His palm slapped the thin wood of the coach door, then swung it open to bang on its hinges.

"Rindo's Station!"

Billy Teachout came out carrying a paintbrush and a bucket half full of axle grease. Ross and Katie were already outside.

"You're late," Billy told the driver.

Ernie Ball pulled a dull gold watch from his vest pocket. "Seven minutes! That's the earliest I've been late." He replaced the watch and dipped a thumb and forefinger daintily into the grease bucket, then twirled the tips of his mustache between the fingers.

"Ross, how are you? Katie, honey." He touched his hat brim to the girl.

Ross Corsen was looking past the stage driver to the man coming out of the coach—the familiar black broadcloth suit and flat-crowned hat. The man reached the ground and there it was, the bland expression, the carefully trimmed mustache. He carried a leather business case tightly and carefully under his arm.

W. F. Sellers. Field supervisor. Southwest Area. Bureau of Indian Affairs.

"Fifteen minutes," Ernie Ball was saying, "for those going on. Time enough for a drink if the innkeeper's feelin' right. Hey, Billy!" His voice changed as he turned to Sellers. "End of the line for you and your friend."

Another man was out of the coach. He stepped down uncertainly and moved next to Sellers. Two others came down, squinting at the glare—thin-lipped, sun-darkened men in range clothes. They stretched and looked about idly, then moved beyond the back of the stage, walking the stiffness from their legs.

Sellers had not taken his eyes from Corsen.

"I thought you might have had the politeness of staying to meet your successor."

Corsen looked at the other man now. "Mr. Verbiest," he said, "I hope you know what you're doing."

"I've instructed Mr. Verbiest on how the agency should be run," Sellers said.

"Then you both ought to make a nice profit," Billy Teachout said mildly.

Sellers stared at him narrowly. "All we want from you is a couple of horses."

"What for?"

"None of your damn business."

Verbiest said, smiling, "We're riding north to the San Carlos Agency. I'd like to take a look at how a smooth-running reservation operates."

"Sellers'll learn you without riding way up there," Ernie Ball said. "All you need is some spare weights to heavy your scale for when you're passing out the 'Paches their beef." Ernie laughed and looked at Teachout. "Hey, Billy?"

"You're insinuating something that could get you into a great deal of trouble in court," Sellers told the stage driver.

"Insinuatin'!"

Sellers turned on Billy Teachout. "I said two horses. Good ones!"

"I'm not the stable hand. Wait for Delgado or get them yourself."

Sellers's face showed no reaction. But he said quietly, "Mr. Teachout, you're through here—as of the next time I get to Prescott."

The station agent shrugged. "While I'm waiting, I'll go inside and pour drinks for those that wants."

Corsen relaxed, exhaling slowly, and watched them all go inside. It was a relief not to have to put up with Sellers anymore. Just seeing him had made his stomach tighten. He glanced at Katie.

"This is a poor way to say good-bye."

"For how long, Ross?"

"Maybe a few months."

The screen door slammed. Corsen remembered the two men in range clothes then. They must have just gone in. Then he was looking at Katie, at the expression changing on her face, eyes alive, looking at something behind him. He turned sharply.

Standing a few feet away was one of the men in range clothes. He stood with his legs spread, as if bracing himself, a short man in faded Levi's, holding a pistol dead on Corsen's stomach.

★

Chapter Three

"Raise your hands up." He motioned with the pistol. "You too, honey." He came forward slowly.

"I'm not armed," Corsen said.

"Take your coat off and drop it."

Corsen took off the worn buckskin and let it fall. He backed up as the man motioned with the pistol, then watched him trample on the coat to make certain there was no gun in it.

"Inside now," the man said.

His partner stood one legged, his left boot on a chair, leaning slightly, elbow on knee, hand holding the pistol idly.

Billy Teachout was behind the bar. Ernie Ball, Sellers, and Verbiest stood in front of it, all with their arms raised. Three pistols were on the floor, along with the business case Sellers had been carrying. Ygenia, Delgado's wife, stood in the kitchen doorway, unable to move.

The one on the chair waved Ross and Katie toward the others. They moved across the room and stood by the front window. "Buz," he said then, "round up that Mexican. He's outside somewhere."

Ernie Ball was squinting at the gunman. "Your face is starting to ring a bell, but your name don't register."

"How would you know my name?"

"You entered Ed Fisher in the book when you paid your fare at Thomas."

The gunman shrugged. "That'll do. . . . What're you carrying this trip?"

"Mail."

"That all?"

"Swear to God. It's on the rack if you want to look."

The one called Buz came in through the kitchen, pushing past the Mexican woman.

"He ain't in sight. Not anywhere."

Corsen glanced out at the yard. Just the stage was there. The horses had been taken away, but the change team had not yet been harnessed.

"That's all right," Fisher said. "Hand me your gun and go through their pockets. We got to move."

He watched Buz search them, stuffing bills and coins into his pockets as he went along. "About how much?" he asked when he had finished.

"Not more than a hundred and fifty."

"What about that satchel there?" He pointed to the business case on the floor.

★ ★ ★

INSTANTLY SELLERS said, "Those are government papers!" More calmly he said, "Bureau statistics."

Ed Fisher said, "Buz, open it up."

The gunman lifted the case and looked at Fisher with surprise. "If there's writin' in here, it's cut on stone." He carried it to the table and unfastened the straps and opened it. He brought out something folded in newspaper and unwrapped it carefully. A leather pouch. He pulled the thongs quickly, eagerly, and dumped the pouch upside-down on the table. The coins came out in a shower.

"Ed! Mint silver!"

Fisher was grinning at Sellers. "How much, Buz?"

"Four, five, six pouches . . . about two thousand!"

Corsen was looking out of the window. There was something, a movement high up on the slope. Then, hearing Buz, he glanced quickly at Sellers. That was it, plain enough. Sellers didn't make that kind of money with a Bureau job. It could only come from selling Indian rations. But now, as the others watched Buz at the table, Corsen's eyes narrowed, looking out into the glare again, and now he could make out the movement. Far out, coming down from the slope, reaching the flat stretch now, were tiny specks, dots against the sand glare that he knew were riders. They were coming from where he had seen Bonito that morning, and suddenly, abruptly, Corsen realized who the riders were.

Ed Fisher was saying, "Get two horses and run off the others. One's saddled already." He looked at the men in front of him. "Whose mount is that in the shed, the chestnut?"

Corsen looked from the window as the screen door slammed behind Buz going out. "The chestnut's mine," he said.

"Thanks for the use."

"You're not going anywhere."

Fisher looked at him quickly, then smiled, his eyes going to Katie. "If you want to play Mister Brave for your girl, wait for when I got more time."

"It's not me that's stopping you," Corsen said, "but I'll tell you again—you're not going anywhere."

"You can talk plainer than that."

"All right. Call to your partner."

"What'll that prove?"

"Just see if he's still there."

Fisher, yelled, "Hey—Buz!"

There was a silence, then boot scuffing and Buz was at the door. "What?"

Fisher looked at Corsen, then back to Buz. "Nothing. Hurry up."

Buz looked at him queerly and moved off again.

"Now what?" Fisher said.

"It'll come," Corsen said. "He hasn't seen them yet."

"Seen who?"

And there it was, as if answering his question—the sound of running, boots on packed sand. Buz's voice yelling, hoarse with panic. Then he was at the door, stumbling against it. " *'Paches!*"

★　★　★

"STAY WHERE YOU ARE!" Fisher held his pistol on the men at the bar and backed toward the door. He glanced out. "How many?"

"Six of them! Let me in!"

"Keep watching!"

Through the window Corsen could now see the cluster of riders plainly, walking their ponies. They were in no hurry—not six, but five, coming across the flat stretch.

"They're peaceful." It was Sellers who said this. "There hasn't been a war party around here in over a year."

Corsen looked at him. "They're twenty miles off the reservation."

"They've been known to wander, but when they do, they have to be taught a lesson. That was your trouble, Corsen—too easy on them. Verbiest, you come along with me and see how it's done."

Corsen said quietly, "Bonito doesn't learn very fast."

"Bonito?" Sellers showed surprise. "He's down in the Madres."

"He wasn't this morning when I talked to him."

"And you're just now telling me?"

"I was fired."

Fisher glanced out the door again, then back, his eyes stopping on Sellers. "Have you got something to do with them?"

Sellers did not answer, but Teachout said, "He's with the Bureau of Indian Affairs."

"Then this is your party, mister," Fisher said, looking at Sellers.

"I'm not obligated to confront known hostiles. That's common sense."

Fisher moved out of the doorway. "You don't have a choice. Get out there and find out what they want." He waved the long-barreled pistol. "Come on, all of you except the women. They stay here."

In the yard Corsen glanced back once at the two outlaws in the doorway. Then they had reached the adobe wall and his gaze swung back to the five Mescaleros who had reined in a hundred paces beyond the wall.

Bonito was a pony's length ahead of the others. He did not resemble the man Corsen had talked to earlier. The flop-brimmed hat was gone and now his coarse face was paint-streaked—a line of ochre from ear to ear crossing the bridge of his nose, another over his chin. His headband was yellow, bright against long hair glistening with oil. Only one thing about him was the same—the Maynard across his lap.

Behind him were Bil-Clin, chief at the Pinaleño Agency, Bil-Clin's son, Sunshine, and two other Indians. All four were armed with old-model carbines.

Corsen's eyes remained on the Mescaleros, but he said to Sellers, "Let's see you go out and teach them a lesson."

Sellers did not reply at first. He kept his eyes on the five Apaches, waiting, expecting them to make a move. Then he said, "All right. Ask him what he wants."

Corsen hesitated. He wanted to make it hard for Sellers, not offer any assistance, but there was Katie and the others to think of. He boosted himself over the wall, then motioned to the Apaches to come on.

They moved forward, Bonito still in the lead, and when they were less than ten feet from the wall Bonito raised his arm and they stopped there. "Cor-sen, we speak to each other again."

"But this time not by accident."

"You told me before that you were not with this one now." Bonito's eyes shifted to Sellers.

"These are not ordinary circumstances," Corsen answered. "Tell me why you are here and I'll relate it to him."

Bonito waited, then nodded toward Sellers. "There is the reason."

"What would you have me tell him?"

"Tell him that he will come with us, until *pesh-e-gar*—many of them—are brought here tomorrow."

"Rifles!"

"Enough for as many of us that could stand in line from here to the house there. And many bullets for the *pesh-e-gar*. This one"—he nodded again to Sellers—"will remain with us until they are brought and the ones who bring them depart again. Then he will be released and my people will go with me from Pinaleño across the Bravos and there we will fight the *Nakai-yes*."

Corsen turned to the others. "He says he needs guns to make war on the Mexicans." Then to Bonito. "You would, of course, not use the guns on this side of the Bravos."

Bonito nodded solemnly.

"The guns would have to be acquired at Fort

Thomas. How do you know the Army would let you have them? Perhaps this man isn't worth a hundred rifles."

Bonito's face barely moved as he spoke. "Killing this one would be a reward in itself."

Corsen paused. "What if he refuses to go with you?"

"At Pinaleño you would find only the women and the children." He turned his head, indicating the dense pines of the higher slope. "The warriors are here, Cor-sen. You are six. Then two men in the house and two women. If he does not come with us, then we will come into your house there—"

Corsen concealed his surprise. "You observe our number well."

Bonito said, "I have been here longer than a full day, waiting for this time. And you see I did not count the Mexican man. He has agreed to remain with us until this one comes to take his place."

Corsen glanced at Billy Teachout. "He says they've got Delgado."

"Oh-my-God—"

Sellers moved closer to Corsen.

"What else does he want?"

"He wants you."

"Me!"

"We get you back in exchange for about a hundred rifles," Corsen added. "I don't know what makes him think you're worth that many."

"Tell him," Sellers said evenly, "that if he doesn't get back to Pinaleño by sundown he'll be shot. Along with Bil-Clin and his boy."

"Pinaleño has moved here," Corsen answered. "The braves are up in the pines. If you don't go with them they'll swarm down all over us."

"They wouldn't get across the wall," Sellers sneered. "There aren't a dozen rifles among the pack of them."

"You forgot, we don't have any."

Sellers was silent. Then, "All right. When the stage doesn't arrive at Gila Ford this evening they'll know something's wrong and send help."

Corsen said, "There are three men at the Gila Ford Station."

"Then they'll get more help!" Sellers said angrily.

"In what—three or four days?"

"What's the matter?" Sellers taunted. "You scared?"

Corsen ignored the remark. "What about Delgado?"

Sellers shrugged. "One thing at a time. Tell him we'll go back and think it over, and let him know."

Corsen told him, and as they were turning to go he looked at Bil-Clin. "Now the chief of the Mescaleros follows the words of a bandit."

Bil-Clin shifted his eyes and did not reply.

★

Chapter Four

Katie came out from the kitchen, edging by Buz, who was in the doorway, and went to Corsen. She had served them food and had now finished washing the dishes. Corsen was at the front window, looking off to the east, watching for a movement to change the monotony of the plain.

She stood close to him and he asked in a low voice, "How's Ygenia?"

"She's praying."

He wanted to say something consoling that she could take to Ygenia, but there was nothing. The Apaches had Delgado. They would keep him until Sellers turned himself over to them. And that was not likely to happen.

★ ★ ★

KATIE'S FACE was close to his. Serious, searching eyes repeating the question he could not answer.

She had been in the kitchen most of the time and she did not know all that had happened since the men had returned. Fisher was in the doorway, a silhouette against the faint outside dusk. Buz was by the kitchen door, holding his gun on the others at the bar end of the room, keeping an eye on Billy Teachout, who was in the kitchen watching the corral and yard.

"Ross, why doesn't he force Sellers to go to the Indians?"

"Fisher would have to shoot him first," Ross said quietly. "This business about the rifles is the long chance. Bonito would like to have them, but I think he'd just as soon have Sellers—for one long day. Sellers knows it. You can't force him to go. No matter what he's stolen, he's a white man. Handing him to Bonito wouldn't be right."

"How long will he wait, Ross?"

"Bonito? He'll send us a message tonight, most likely. And if we don't act on it he'll come at sunup."

"The outlaw would have to give you guns then," Katie said.

Corsen nodded. "He's holding off as long as he can, waiting for a miracle. I feel kind of sorry for him. He can't fight off Bonito with just one man, but if he gives us guns he's through. He loses either way."

They were silent then, standing close to each other.

Corsen's gaze would come in from the dim plain and go about the room.

Fisher, in the doorway, glanced now and then at Sellers. You have to give him credit, Corsen thought. Sitting on the edge of his nerves until the last possible minute.

Buz looks hard, but he leans on Fisher. He could never do this alone. They thought they had something good, and it turns out to be the worst jackpot they could fall into. Let them stew in it.

Billy and Ernie are men who know patience because they do more than just live here: they're part of the country. They'll sit through something like this and not show it.

Verbiest is afraid to open his mouth. His voice would give him away. He's so scared, he can taste it.

And Sellers. He'll never believe he's through— and maybe he isn't. He's got his life at stake, plus a government post and two thousand dollars in government silver. The money must have come from selling agency stores. He'll scheme, confident that he'll think of something to pull him out of this.

Bonito has nothing to lose. With a hundred warriors, and nothing to lose, he will probably win.

Strips of gray light crossed the room from the

doorway and the windows. Outside, the moonlight showed the station yard in dim, unmoving stillness, bounded by the adobe wall, a pale line against the darkness beyond. Corsen looked out of the window again, then moved toward Fisher. He saw the dull gleam of a pistol barrel bear on him and he said, "Ed. A word with you."

"Come ahead," Fisher said quietly.

"It'll be dark in a few minutes," Corsen said. "You'd better give us our guns."

"I'll take my chances for a while."

"You won't be able to watch us in the dark—and you're not going to use a lamp with Bonito outside."

Fisher was silent. Then, "I'm trying to think it out," he said wearily.

"You don't have a choice," Corsen told him. "Those are Mescaleros. You're old enough to know how they behave when they're up."

"No, I don't. Not the way I know what would happen if you people had guns. Buz and I would turn our backs once—"

"All right," Corsen said. "Then give back all the money you took."

"Tell them I was just kiddin', eh?"

"I'm thinking about two women being here," Corsen said, "and a hundred Mescaleros out there.

Make up your mind one way or the other—but do it before it's too late."

★ ★ ★

THE SOUND CAME to them gradually. It came faintly, growing out of the darkness, at first a muffled sound, now the unmistakable clop of a horse moving at a slow walk. A chair scraped in the room. Fisher's voice rasped, "Quiet!"

In the stillness Fisher cocked his head, listening, then whispered close to Corsen's cheek, "It's stopped."

Corsen waited. "At the gate," he said.

"It's a trick." Fisher was talking to himself. "A damn Apache trick."

"Maybe it is." Corsen paused. "And maybe it isn't, Ed," he said quietly. "If I was to go out there, would you hold your gun that way?"

"You're crazy."

"Let's find out." Corsen pushed through the screen door without a sound and was moving across the yard. He walked unhurriedly, because if Bonito was behind the wall, running would not make a difference; the yard was open, and gray with moonlight. He reached the gate and stood with his hand on the heavy latch.

Fisher watched him tensely. He felt someone close to him and glanced to see the girl. Billy Teachout was behind her. They looked at Fisher, then out toward the gate, and they did not speak.

In the darkness someone said, "What is it?" excitedly.

At a window Ernie Ball's voice hissed. "Shhhhh!"

They watched Corsen lift the iron latch. Then the shadowy figure pushed against the gate and the squeak of the hinges was a mournful screech with no other sounds in the night. Corsen went through the opening, and for the moment he was out of sight Katie held her breath. Then the gate swung wide and he was there again, leading the larger, darker shadow of a horse. A rider was atop the horse, head down, swaying gently with the movement of the horse's shoulders and flanks. Corsen closed the gate and came on, holding the horse close under the muzzle by a hackamore.

"Who is it?" from inside the doorway.

Fisher was in the yard now. He looked at Corsen, then toward the rider, questioningly.

Corsen went to the rider, raised his arms, and said gently, "Come, *viejo*." The small figure toppled hesitantly, stiffly, into Corsen's arms.

He heard someone behind him say, "Delgado—"

They carried him inside to a bedroom and eased him down onto the bed. And when the lamp was lighted next to the bed, no one recognized Delgado.

"Mary, Virgin and Mother," Ygenia said, close to Delgado's cheek, kneeling on the floor and stroking her hand gently over his head. When Katie came in with a basin of water, she mopped his face, washing the blood away. She moved the cloth over his eyes very gently and when she took it away she gasped and uttered the name of the Mother of God again.

Delgado's face was knife scarred, small marks crisscrossing his cheeks. His nose was broken, that was evident, and his right eye was no longer in the socket.

His head came off the blanket, then fell back as the thin lines of his face tightened. He said, almost inaudibly, "Ross."

"I'm here," Corsen said close to his cheek. "Don't talk now. Say it in the morning."

Delgado breathed. "Bonito did this to me. There were others who beat at me and stuck me with their knives, but it was Bonito who did this." His hand waved close to his face.

"As I gathered the fresh team, one of them broke away and I went after it afoot because this one was a friend and would come if I approached with gentleness. But this time he went a greater distance. When he was near the piñon he stopped and let me approach, and at that moment the barbarians came from out of the pines. Almost as if this friend had lured me to them—"

✷ ✷ ✷

CORSEN SAID GENTLY, "Tell this in the morning."

Delgado turned his head, opening his left eye. "If you are here to listen." He waved his hand again. "Bonito did this to me. He impressed upon me that when he comes he will take the remainder of my sight. I would not like that to happen. He said that you had failed him. Now he will enter this house with the coming of the sun. . . ."

Silence then. Corsen rose as Ygenia began to stroke Delgado's head. Fisher appeared in the doorway.

"Your guns are on the table," he said quietly.

✷

Chapter Five

Corsen pushed his gun belt lower on his hips and picked up the Winchester leaning against the support post. He heard the screen door close softly and peered into the darkness around the coach which they had pushed into the stable shed. A figure was moving along the front of the house toward him.

It was Fisher. "There better be two of us out here. The east side of the house is a blind spot. And when the shootin' starts," he added, "I don't hanker to be in the same room with that thievin' government man. He could swing his barrel two feet and let go, easy as not." He looked at Corsen's carbine and holstered pistol. "You had them out here?"

"With the saddle," Corsen said.

"Where's your horse? It was here."

"I took it around to the corral. I'd rather have it run off than hit."

They rolled straw bales from the back wall of the shed to the front and piled them three high for some protection. There were no doors on the stable shed. It was built out from the station house four wagons wide. Ernie's coach was in the first stall nearest the house. Corsen went to the small window at the far end of the shed and Fisher stopped near him, looking out into the night.

"Might they come before dawn?"

"I've never heard of it," Corsen answered. "But don't put that down in your book as a rule. Bonito might have told Delgado dawn to put us off guard."

"That was something, what he did to him."

Corsen said quietly, "Delgado was lucky. Bonito's

showing off. He wants us to think he's got full control of the situation. Even to letting a prisoner go, knowing he'll get him back again."

"He could convince me."

"I'm not so sure he has." Corsen paused. "If I could talk to Bil-Clin—I don't see how he could help but resent this renegade's coming up and taking over. If we could get Bil-Clin alone. . . ."

Fisher said nothing.

Sometimes when you wait, the time goes slow, Corsen thought, but now it is going fast, so fast it isn't time anymore, but something else. That was a month ago that I told Katie I would come and get her. And Billy was surprised because he hadn't known what was going on. It seems like a month, but it was yesterday afternoon. Now he pictured himself with Katie at night, her face in soft shadows. She was in the room with Ygenia and Delgado, and a pistol. The door was bolted. If they broke through the door, then she would fire the pistol until it was empty. Then, in a timeless time she would pray. Pray that it would not take long for Ygenia and for herself. She would not use the gun on herself to make it quick. Even if he had asked her to, she would not. She doesn't even show this. There may be a little of it in her eyes, but it isn't in her voice. You're lucky, Ross. But how can you be lucky and unlucky at the same time?

But now more time had passed and there was an orange streak in the east and the sky was no longer full dark, and suddenly shadows were coming over the wall. Shadows that were the shapes of men, but without sound and without the gleam of weapons. They dropped and clung close to the wall. Now some were coming forward!

"Oh, my God!" Fisher had seen them.

From the house, "They're coming!" and the hurried report of a rifle. A pause, now a staccato of rifle fire and suddenly the station yard erupted into wild sound—whining gun reports and the full-throated scream of the Mescalero war cry and the whinnying of horses.

Down the carbine barrel Corsen squinted at three warriors coming zigzagging toward the shed. Then the outside two were out of vision and he fired. The Mescalero fell in his tracks. As he levered, the other two tuned abruptly and were back to the wall as he aimed again. One of them was on the wall, and he brought the barrel up an inch and squeezed the trigger, and the warrior dropped to the other side. The third one was over, out of sight. And as suddenly as the firing had started, it stopped.

Corsen glanced both ways, surprised. Two, three, four of them were down and the rest had retreated. They're feeling us out, he thought. Seeing how many guns we have.

Fisher exhaled a long sigh. "We drove them off."

"The first time," Corsen said. "Now Bonito knows what we have and he'll scratch his head till something comes out of it."

Fisher looked up suddenly. "There!"

It was the Apache Corsen had hit first, now crawling toward the wall, dragging his left leg. Fisher raised his pistol.

"Hold it!" Corsen squinted hard at the Apache. "That's Bil-Clin's boy!"

Corsen waited until Sunshine reached the wall. Then, as the Apache raised himself slowly, painfully, with his weight on his right leg, Corsen raised the carbine and fired.

The bullet sang, ricocheting off the wall, and white dust spattered above the boy's head as he sank down.

Corsen levered a shell into the breech, his eyes on Sunshine. Watch him. Watch him like a hawk. He's got a broken leg, but he can be over that wall in one jump.

The next moment Sunshine was pushing up with his arms and his one good leg. But it was a feint, for

he lunged suddenly to the side. Corsen was ready.
He swung the barrel and placed the next shot a foot
in front of Sunshine. Pieces of adobe splattered on
the Apache's hair, and now he sat down and stared
toward the shed.

Corsen said, "Watch along the wall, Ed. I'm going out. You edge toward the house."

Fisher said, "What?"

"If this works," Corsen said hurriedly, "I'll give
you a signal. When I do, bring the men out. Just
the men!"

Sunshine had not moved, and now Corsen said,
"Here we go." He handed the Winchester to
Fisher and pushed over the straw bales. Going over
them, he drew his pistol and walked out into the
open yard with the handgun pointed toward Sunshine. When he was in the middle of the yard he
stopped.

"Bil-Clin!"

There was no answer, though he knew they were
on the other side of the wall.

He shouted again, "Bil-Clin!" Then he said in
Spanish, "My gun is on your son!" His eyes shifted
above Sunshine. Stillness. A bare line of adobe—
and then Bil-Clin was standing a dozen paces to the
left, head and shoulders above the wall. Corsen's
eyes went to him.

"Come over the wall."

Bil-Clin's arms came up and he raised himself to the top of the wall and dropped to the inside. He did not look at his son, but approached Corsen.

"Bil-Clin," Corsen said, "call Bonito and the others."

The Apache said a word in Mescalero and suddenly his warriors were at the wall. They had stood up and were now a line of bare chests and war paint and thick blue-black hair with cloth bands over the foreheads. Bonito stood among them, but he was alone. He lifted his Maynard and rested it on the wall.

"Come in, Bonito," Corsen said. And when the renegade did not move he glanced at Bil-Clin, then cocked his pistol. "Order him to come in—if you're still the chief."

Bil-Clin looked at his son now, for the first time. The boy's eyes, between stripes of yellow paint, were on Corsen. Bil-Clin spoke again in Mescalero and it was evident that his words were for Bonito. But Bonito did not answer.

Corsen tightened. He could feel it in his stomach, but he made his voice sound calm. "Bonito, you are now chief?"

Still the Apache said nothing.

"Yesterday you told me that chieftainship of the

Mescalero is not a thing of heredity, but a position earned by the one most capable in war. In fighting. So, Bonito, are you chief?"

Bonito did not move. Corsen was looking at him now, but he glanced away momentarily toward Ed Fisher, and nodded to him.

"Let me tell you something, Bonito. There are others who live here now—some with authority that seems to contradict yours. How can you be a chief if you have opposed only this old man, Bil-Clin?"

★ ★ ★

HE GLANCED TOWARD the house and saw them coming out now.

"What about the government man, Bonito? He tells me you are a woman—a filthy pig of a woman with the diseases of animals. Unfit to live. And he has much authority. Perhaps he is the true chief here?"

Bonito's eyes had gone to Sellers as he appeared in the doorway. The eyes held on the man, narrowing, and then Bonito was over the wall.

"How would you have it, Cor-sen?"

"Whatever is customary."

"With the knife, then."

"I'll tell him." Corsen turned to the men in front of the station house. "Sellers, Bonito says you're afraid to fight him alone."

Sellers was startled. "You're crazy!"

"Ask him."

"Fight him with what?"

"Knives."

"Now I know you're crazy."

"You want to convince him you're boss, don't you? Beat him in a fair fight, the way they have to pick their chiefs sometimes."

Fisher moved a step toward Sellers and, as he did so, brought the Winchester up and down in a short motion and Sellers's pistol was out of his hand. He looked at Fisher with complete surprise, watching the outlaw pick up the pistol.

"I'll hold it for you while you're teaching that red son a lesson."

"Corsen! Tell him I won't fight him, that we don't do this in our government."

"Bonito," Corsen translated, "he says he does not have a knife."

★ ★ ★

Bonito reached behind him and drew a dull-gleaming blade from his waistband. His arm swung low. The knife scraped, bouncing over the sand to stop near Sellers.

"Corsen, tell that savage—"

"Listen," Corsen said, "this started because of you and Bonito. So you and he are going to finish it."

"He's fought this way all of his life. I wouldn't have a chance!"

Corsen shrugged. "You can't tell."

Bonito was handed a knife and without hesitating he stepped toward Sellers.

Fisher stooped, picked up the knife at Sellers's feet, and put it in his hand. "If you make it, I'll buy you a drink."

"Wait a minute, Ross!" Sellers backed up. "Ross, tell him I won't do it—"

But Bonito was in front of him now.

The Mescalero lowered his head, hunching his shoulders, and brought the knife up in front of him, looking up at Sellers's face through half-closed eyes.

"Ross!"

The blade flashed, a short swipe of naked arm that was out and in before anyone could see what had happened.

Sellers screamed. His left cheek was slashed from ear to mouth.

"Ross!"

Bonito feinted toward Sellers's head. Going back, Sellers brought up his arm, but the blade dropped. It flashed low under his guard and flicked a short arc across the sucked-in stomach. Sellers's vest opened from pocket to pocket and he screamed again and this time turned and started to run. But he came up short, pushed, jolted back to face Bonito by Teachout, who stood behind him.

"You're going the wrong way," Teachout said.

"Let me go!"

Bonito stood waiting.

Corsen's gaze went from him to Sellers. "Are you through?"

Sellers, blood smeared over his face, was breathing hard, holding his stomach. "Ross." He gasped. "Shoot him! Now, while he's still!"

"Are you quitting?" Corsen said.

"God! Shoot him!"

Corsen said calmly, "Fight him, or else get out."

Sellers looked at him strangely, taken by surprise. "Get out?"

"That's right. Ride out of here and take Verbiest with you. Forget you ever worked for the Bureau. There are seven people here to testify you're not fit for the job. Now, either fight him or write yourself off."

Sellers hesitated, fingering the cut across his stomach, his eyes on Corsen. Then his gaze went slowly to Bonito, who stood unmoving, watching him. Gradually Sellers's grip loosened around the knife, and as it dropped from his hand he turned abruptly and walked to the station house. The screen door banged.

"Now," Bonito said coldly, "there is no more doubt."

"It is still in my mind," Corsen said mildly. He lowered the pistol he'd been holding on Sunshine and turned to Bonito. He added, pointedly, "I have seen women fight before. Usually it proves nothing."

Bonito's eyes narrowed. "Say your words straight, Cor-sen."

Corsen stopped a stride from the Apache. He raised his hand and swung the open palm hard against Bonito's face. The Apache was taken off guard and staggered back, but he did not go down.

"Is that straight enough?"

Corsen looked back at Ed Fisher and swung the pistol underhand toward him, and as he turned back to Bonito he shifted his feet suddenly and came around with his right fist smashing against the Apache's face. And this time Bonito went down.

"Maybe that's a little straighter." Then, looking toward Bil-Clin, Corsen said, "Is this your chief?"

Bonito came to one knee. His mouth was half open with numbness, but he smiled and said, "All right. Corsen."

Behind him he heard Fisher say, "Here's the knife." Corsen half turned as if to look at Fisher, but it was a short movement. He pivoted, swinging his left hand, and again caught Bonito on the face as he was rising.

The Apache went down, rolling away from Corsen's reach, but as he came up Corsen was there. He swung a right and then a left to the Apache's head to beat him down again.

Bonito looked up at him, propping himself with his elbows; his face was cut at both eyes and his mouth swollen. And now he considered what to do next—how to fight this man whose not using a weapon was an insult. He brought his knees up under him, then one foot, watching Corsen closely.

Corsen moved a step closer, clenching his fists. Bonito will pull something this time, he thought. Bonito was rising, then suddenly throwing himself at Corsen's legs. Corsen dodged and kicked out, but his boot caught Bonito's shoulder and now the Apache was rolling. Corsen started after him, then stopped dead as Bonito jumped to his feet.

Fisher yelled, "You want it now, Ross?"

Corsen shook his head. This was the way to beat him, if it could be done. He started toward Bonito, thinking: Carry it to him. Once he starts calling the play, you're through. Watch his eyes. They'll tell you a snap second before he moves. He moved close to Bonito, tensed, watching the yellow-filmed eyes, smelling the animal smell of the man, seeing the eyes now and not the face.

Corsen drew his arm back slowly, knotting the fist. He shifted his weight suddenly, swinging the fist—*the eyes*—then just as suddenly threw himself to the side. Bonito's knife jabbed viciously, but Corsen was not there. And as the Apache came around to find him, in that split second Corsen was ready. He went back on his left foot, his body balanced, and then his weight shifted and his boot kicked savagely into Bonito's loins. The Apache gasped and stopped dead in his tracks, bending, holding his stomach.

And that was it. Corsen hit him with one fist, then the other, and as Bonito started to sag he caught the Apache's arm and drove his right fist straight into the paint-streaked face. The Apache went down, dropping the knife, and landed heavily on his back.

"There, Bil-Clin, is your chief," Corsen said. He went over to Sunshine and knelt beside him, examining the shinbone that his bullet had broken.

Bil-Clin was standing next to him now. It was hard for him to speak, even if it was not an outright apology, for he was Mescalero, but he said, "What would you have us do?"

Corsen rose and looked at Bil-Clin. "If you wish, we will get an American doctor for your son. But now go back to Pinaleño and take your dead."

"And you will come, Cor-sen?"

★ ★ ★

CORSEN'S GAZE went over the line of Apaches at the wall. Immobile faces, streaks of vermilion and bright yellow, and looking at them he was angry. But he thought: These are Mescaleros. You know what they are. You know what they can do. You were lucky today, but don't push your luck, and perhaps because of it make some cavalry patrol officer, who isn't even out here yet, push his. And he nodded slowly, wearily, to Bil-Clin and said, "Yes. I will come."

The others were standing almost in a line. Teachout and Ernie Ball, Ed Fisher and his partner and Verbiest.

Maybe this will straighten Fisher out, Corsen thought. He's a man you'd buy a drink for, even after he's robbed you. Verbiest made a mistake, but he knows it and he won't make it again. . . .

And then he did not think of them anymore. Katie was in the doorway and he walked toward the house.

4

No Man's Guns

As HE DREW near the mass of tree shadows that edged out to the road he heard the voice, the clear but hesitant sound of it coming unexpectedly in the almost-dark stillness.

"Cliff—"

His right knee touched the booted Springfield and he thought of it calmly, instinctively, drawing it left-handed in his mind, as he slowed the sorrel to a walk. Now at the edge of the shadows he saw a man with a rifle.

The man called uncertainly, "Cliff?"

"You got the wrong party," he answered, and neck-reined the sorrel toward the trees.

Less than twenty feet away the rifle came up suddenly. "Who are you?"

"My name's Mitchell."

The rifle barrel hung hesitantly. "You better light down."

Astride the McClellan saddle, Dave Mitchell didn't move. He sat with his shoulders pulled back, yet he was relaxed. Narrow hips, sun-darkened, thin-lined features beneath the slightly turned-up forward brim of a faded Stetson and everything about him said *Cavalry*. Everything but the rough-wool gray suit he wore. His coat was unbuttoned and his dark shirt was unmistakably Army issue.

"You're camped back in there?" Mitchell asked, and he was thinking, watching the man studying him: I'm the wrong man and now he doesn't know what to do. The man with the rifle didn't reply and Mitchell said, "I'm ready to camp the night. If you already got a place, maybe I could join you."

For a moment the man didn't answer. Then the rifle, a long-barreled Remington, waved in a short arc. "Light down."

Mitchell let his right rein fall as he came off the sorrel. The rifle waved again. The man stood aside and Mitchell walked past him leading the sorrel. They moved through the trees, thinly scattered aspen, then cottonwood as the ground began to slope gradually, and Mitchell knew there'd be a creek close by. Unexpectedly, then, he saw the broad clearing and a wagon illuminated by firelight.

The ribbed canvas covering of it formed a pale background for the two figures who stood watching him approach. A man, his legs slightly apart and his hand covering the butt of a holstered revolver. A woman was next to him and she watched Mitchell with open curiosity as he entered the clearing.

"Rady's brought us a guest," the woman said.

The man with the rifle was next to Mitchell now. "Hyatt, he says he wants to camp." The woman walked to the fire, but Hyatt, his hand still on the revolver, didn't move. Nor did he answer, and his eyes remained on Mitchell. "He said he was ready to camp the night," Rady added, "so I thought—"

"Open your coat," Hyatt said. "Hold it open."

Slowly Mitchell spread the coat open. "I'm not armed."

"He's got a carbine on the horse," Rady said.

Hyatt glanced at him. "Go back where you were."

*   *   *

MITCHELL DROPPED the rein and walked toward the low-burning fire as the woman extended a porcelain cup toward him and said, "Coffee?" Behind him he heard Rady's footsteps in the dry leaves, then fading to nothing, and he felt Hyatt watching him as he took the cup of coffee, his hand momentarily touching the woman's.

"You drink your coffee, then move off," Hyatt said. He was in his early thirties, but a week-old beard stubble darkened his face, adding ten years to his appearance. His face was drawn into tight, sunken cheeks and he looked as if he'd never smiled in his life. To the woman he said, "I'll tell you when we start giving coffee to everybody who goes by."

Mitchell hesitated, letting the sudden tension inside him subside, and he thought, Don't let him rile you. Don't even tell him to go to hell. He said to Hyatt, "I'll leave in a minute."

"You'll leave sooner if I say so."

Maybe you ought to tell him, at that, Mitchell thought. Just to see what he'd do. But he heard the woman say, "Hy, don't talk like that," and he turned to the fire again.

"You shut your mouth!" Hyatt told her.

Mitchell sipped his coffee, his eyes on the woman. Her face was lit by the firelight and it shone warmly and cleanly. He watched her glance at Hyatt but not answer him and he said to her, mildly, "I don't want to start a family argument."

"We'll ignore him, then," the woman said. She smiled and the smile was faintly in her eyes. She'd impressed Mitchell as a woman who smiled little, and the soft radiance that came briefly into her eyes surprised him. Still, she fell into a type in Mitchell's mind: small, frail looking, a woman who picked at her food yet was strong and you wondered what kept her going. Light hair, thin, delicately formed features, and dark shadows beneath the eyes. A serious kind, a woman who loved strongly and simply. A woman who spoke little. This, Mitchell believed, was the most interesting type of all. The most feminine, even while sometimes reminding you of a little boy. At least the most appealing. Perhaps the kind to marry.

She said, "Could I ask where you're going?"

"Home," Mitchell answered. No, she didn't exactly fit the type. She talked too freely.

"Where is that?"

"Banderas. I just left Whipple Barracks yesterday. Discharged."

"I thought so," the woman said. "Just the way you stand."

"I suppose some of it's bound to rub off, after twelve years."

"You don't look that old."

"Older'n you. I'm almost thirty-one."

"Were you an officer?"

"No, ma'am. Sergeant."

"You're going home to your folks?"

"Yes, ma'am. My dad has a place near Banderas."

"They'll be glad to see you."

Mitchell half turned as Hyatt said, "How do we know you're from Whipple?"

"I just told you I was."

"What proof you got?"

"I don't have to show you anything."

Hyatt's hand hung close to his holster. "You don't think so, huh?"

"Look," Mitchell said. "Why don't you quit standing on your nerves."

"Let's see your proof," Hyatt said.

Mitchell glanced at the woman. "You ought to keep him locked up."

The woman half smiled. "Do you have discharge papers?"

Mitchell's hand slipped into his open coat and patted his shirt pocket. "Right here."

"Why don't you show him?" the woman said. "So we'll have a little peace."

★ ★ ★

MITCHELL SHOOK his head. "It's a matter of principle now." A matter of principle. And a matter of twelve years someone telling you what to do. You can take it when you're being paid to take it. But this one isn't paying, Mitchell thought. Take that handgun off him and bend it over his head? No, just get out. You don't have any business here.

The woman said, "Men are always talking about principle, or honor."

"Well, I'm through talking about it tonight," Mitchell said. He handed the empty cup to her. "Much obliged. I'm moving on now." She looked at him, but said nothing.

He saw her eyes shift suddenly.

Behind you!

It snapped in his mind and he heard the movement and he wheeled, bringing up his arms, throwing himself low at Hyatt who was almost on top of him. His shoulder slammed into Hyatt's knees and he drove forward as the pistol barrel came down against his spine. His arms clamped Hyatt's legs and he came up suddenly, His boots digging into the sand, throwing Hyatt's legs over his shoulder. Hyatt landed on his back, rolling over almost as he struck the ground, frantically reaching for the revolver knocked from his hand, almost touching it as Mitchell dropped on top of him.

They rolled in the sand, Hyatt's fingers tearing through Mitchell's shirt, clawing at his throat.

Mitchell's hand found the revolver. He threw it spinning across the sand and his fist came back to slam against Hyatt's face. He pushed himself free, rolling, rising to his feet, and as Hyatt came up he swung hard against his jaw. Hyatt staggered. He started to go down and Mitchell hit him again, holding him momentarily with his left hand as his right clubbed into the upturned face. Hyatt's head snapped back and he went down.

Mitchell turned to the woman. He was breathing heavily and his left hand was pressed to the small of his back. "Are you married to him?" he asked.

She shook her head. "Not really."

Mitchell hesitated. If he turned away he'd never see this woman again. Something made him ask, "Do you love him?"

She looked at him, her face softly impassive in the firelight. "You'd better move along," she said quietly.

For a moment Mitchell's eyes remained on her, as if he were reluctant to leave. He turned to the sorrel, then hesitated again and walked over to Hyatt.

"Mister, you brought this on yourself. Your man out there thought I was somebody named Cliff and he brought me in because he was too scared to do anything else. I don't care who you are. . . . I don't care who Cliff is—" Mitchell broke off. "If you want to know the truth, I think you're crazy." He glanced momentarily at the woman before telling Hyatt, "Maybe you got some good points, but if you do you keep them a secret."

Hyatt's head came up slowly. He watched Mitchell go to his sorrel and mount. He watched him silently, his hand covering a folded piece of paper on the ground beneath him. A square of paper folded four times just to fit into a shirt pocket.

Mitchell urged the sorrel into the trees, letting it have its head, but holding it enough to reach the road farther down from where Rady would be. The woman stayed in his mind: standing in the firelight, her eyes meeting his and not lowering even when he continued to stare at her.

Some woman.

★ ★ ★

HIS BODY CAME alive as the shot sounded behind him and his hand instinctively went to the booted carbine. He turned in the saddle drawing the Springfield, the sorrel sidestepping nervously, kicking the dry leaves, throwing its head. There were other sounds in the leaves and suddenly a man's voice: "Throw up your hands!" And almost with the words Mitchell was dragged from the saddle. Men were all around him in the darkness, two holding his arms, and as he tried to rise a fist came from nowhere, stinging hard against his face.

A rifle barrel jabbed into his back and he was taken through the trees, a man holding each arm. There were more men at the clearing and the nearest ones stepped aside as Mitchell was brought in. One man was building the fire. Another was climbing the wagon wheel, now looking inside. The rest stood in a semicircle around Hyatt and the woman.

The man holding Mitchell's left arm shouted, "Dyke, we got the other one!"

Mitchell saw one of the men turn and nod his head, then beckon them to come closer. He stood relaxed, a tall man wearing a stiff-brimmed hat low and straight over his eyes, and a tawny tip-twisted mustache that in the firelight blended with the weathered cut of his features. His coat was open, a dark coat . . . and then Mitchell saw it. The deputy star against the dark cloth and everything was suddenly perfectly clear.

Hyatt was saying, "What're you doing! We're camped here and you barge in, shooting—"

A man said, "You scrambled for that gun quick enough."

"How'd I know who you were?"

"You know now." The man laughed. Mitchell

looked from this man to the others. There were perhaps a dozen in the group, but only Dyke and two
or three more wore deputy stars.

"Listen"—Hyatt's voice calmed—"I think you
could've announced yourselves, that's all. You're
looking for somebody and you want to ask some
questions, that it?"

Dyke shook his head. "I don't have any questions."

Hyatt's eyes shifted along the line of men.
"We're on our way down to Tucson. I'm going in
business with a man down there."

Dyke said nothing. His eyes were on Hyatt,
studying him.

"In the freight business," Hyatt said. "This
man's already got contracts."

"Are you through?" Dyke said then.

Hyatt frowned. "What do you mean?"

"I'll tell a story now," Dyke said. "It starts the
day before yesterday when the Hatch & Hodges
was held up an hour out of Mojave. One of the passengers, Mr. J. A. Hicks, was shot and killed when
he raised an objection. Now, this Mr. Hicks was
owner of the Mogollon Cattle Company—Slash
M—of which I'm foreman. Mr. Hicks, besides being boss, was my best friend . . . which doesn't

mean much to the story aside from it's the reason I was deputized to take out a posse."

Hyatt said, "I'm sorry to hear that, but—"

"I'm not finished," Dyke stated. "You see, these holdup men separated after the robbery. We spent a whole day scratching for sign and finally we got on one we were pretty sure of. Last night we caught up with a man named Cliff something. Now, at first he said he didn't know anything about it."

★ ★ ★

DYKE'S EYES HADN'T left Hyatt's. "I hit this man twice. The second one broke his jaw and after that he wrote down what we wanted to know. How he was to meet his friends tonight, and where. A woman and two men posing as travelers. A man named James Rady; another by the name of Hyatt Earl."

"Well?" Hyatt said. His voice was controlled, and it told nothing of what he might be thinking.

Dyke brought a match out of his vest pocket and wedged it into the corner of his mouth, shaking his head as he did. "That's all there is to the story."

Hyatt hesitated. "Now what?"

"Now, Mr. Earl," Dyke said mildly, his eyes lifting then, "we're going to hang you right on that cottonwood over there."

"What're you talking about, hanging! You don't even know—" Hyatt broke off. He looked at Dyke and at his men and for a long moment he was silent, gaining control of himself. He said then, calmly, almost defiantly, "You got to take us to trial. That's what the law says."

The matchstick moved under Dyke's full mustache. "Mr. Earl, are you telling me what I have to do?"

That was it. The futility of arguing showed briefly on Hyatt's face. He asked, "What about the woman?"

Dyke shook his head. "This Cliff said she didn't want any part of it, but you forced her into it. We're not bothered about her. Just you and Rady there." He nodded directly at Mitchell.

Mitchell frowned. Hurriedly then his eyes swept the clearing. Rady wasn't here! He called to Dyke, "I'm not Rady! He's the one with the Remington . . . was out by the road."

Dyke studied him before answering. "There wasn't anybody out there."

"Then he got away, but I sure as hell ain't Rady!"

"Who're you supposed to be?"

"Dave Mitchell. I just rode in a little while ago looking to camp." He saw Hyatt watching him, a grin softening the dark bearded face.

"Rady," Hyatt said, "are you drunk or something?"

Mitchell stared at him with disbelief. "What's the matter with you? Tell them who I am!"

Hyatt shook his head. "There's no use in that, Rady. Let's own up . . . take our medicine like men."

Mitchell's eyes went to Dyke. "Listen. This man's crazy. I suspected it before. Now I'm sure."

"If I was in your shoes," said Dyke, "I might pull the same stunt."

Mitchell paused. "All right"—his glance went to the woman—"ask her."

She looked at Mitchell, then shook her head. "He's not Rady. His name is Mitchell."

Dyke said, "Uh-huh, and you're Mrs. Mitchell."

"I never saw him before this evening."

"Claire," Hyatt said sympathetically, "there's no use. Rady's got to take his medicine just the same way I do."

The woman's face was cold and showed no emotion. "He had a fight with this man Mitchell and lost. That's why he wants to see him hang."

"Claire! . . . Rady and I were just kidding! You thought we really meant it?"

Mitchell looked at Dyke again. "You said that holdup was day before yesterday. I can prove I was at Whipple then. I was just discharged yesterday."

"What's your proof?" Dyke asked.

"Ask anybody at Whipple!"

"Rady," Hyatt said, "delaying it a few days ain't going to help any, they'll still hang you. Let's get it over with."

Mitchell's expression changed suddenly and his hand went to his chest. "My discharge order! It's dated yesterday!"

"Keep your hand out of that coat!" Dyke snapped. He nodded to one of the men near Mitchell. "Take a look."

The man stepped in front of Mitchell. His hand went over the shirt, then to the inside coat pocket. "Nothing," he said over his shoulder.

Mitchell's hand came up. He felt the empty pocket, and the part of his shirt that was torn—

"Listen, while we were fighting my shirt was ripped. The paper fell out, that's what happened. Look around there, right where you're standing!"

Dyke continued to study Mitchell, but some of his men moved about, looking at the ground and scuffing the sand with their boots. A man said, "I don't see nothin'," and another said, "Not around here." Watching them, the tension building and becoming unbearable. Mitchell suddenly tore himself from the men holding him. They started after him and Dyke called, "Let him go!"

Mitchell came on, his eyes searching the ground, then dropped to his hands and knees, his fingers brushing the sand, smoothing it, and carefully he covered the area where the fight had taken place. He came up slowly and sat back on his heels. "It's not here," he said wearily. Then: "Wait! When I was pulled off my horse—" He came to his feet quickly.

Dyke asked, "You ever on the stage?"

"I'm telling you the truth!" Mitchell screamed. "Can't you see that!"

"I see a man fighting awful hard," Dyke replied, "for a life he don't deserve."

"What do you expect me to do!" Mitchell paused then. He breathed in and out and said, more calmly, "I swear to Almighty God I had nothing to do with that holdup."

"That's what this Cliff said," Dyke answered. "Before I broke his jaw."

"Rady," Hyatt spoke up, "you don't want that to happen to you, do you?"

Mitchell ignored him. Still looking at Dyke he said, "Isn't there a doubt in your mind?" Dyke didn't answer and in the silence their eyes held.

Then, behind Mitchell, a man said, "Let's have

some coffee first." Dyke's eyes lifted. He nodded
and walked toward the fire, finished with Mitchell.

★ ★ ★

HYATT AND THE woman were moved over by the
wagon. Then Mitchell was brought over. They tied
Hyatt's and Mitchell's hands behind their backs
and made them sit down, the woman between them.

There was nothing to be said. In silence they
watched Dyke's men build another fire close to the
cottonwood tree they would use. Two men entered
the clearing carrying riatas, uncoiling them as they
crossed to the tree. Mitchell saw his sorrel and a
bay brought in and the saddles were taken off both
horses.

Now what do you do? he thought.

Tell him!

I did tell him! He's hard-shelled and mean because Hyatt killed his friend and that's all he can
think about. But he's calm about it, isn't he? Judge
and jury wrapped into one hard-bitten weathered
face. His mind is the law and he can be as calm as
he pleases, knowing his way is the only way.

Twelve years of campaigning and you're going to
die under another man's name. Nobody knowing . . . no, two people knowing who you are. The
woman—Claire—and Hyatt.

Two feet away and you can't even touch him. Get up quick and butt his face in with your head! No . . . come on, think straight now. Now isn't a time to think about revenge. Forget about him. You're going to die and that's all there is to it.

He said it in his mind, feeling each word: I'm going to die. More slowly then: I am going to die.

All right, now you know it. You always knew it, but now you know it. Come on, think straight. I *am* thinking straight. Go to hell with that thinking straight business! There's no *straight* way to think when you're going to die. What did you think about the other time? The first and only and supposedly last other time.

Nervous and not liking it, not believing that it was happening to him, but holding himself together nevertheless and thinking over and over again that it was a shame to die alone. Alone, because the Coyotero tracker didn't count. You couldn't talk about last things in sign language. Dos Fuegos had taken out a buckskin pouch in which he carried his *hoddentin,* the sacred pollen made from tule that would ward off evil, and with that he had readied himself.

★ ★ ★

Corporal Mitchell then, Corporal Mitchell and a Coyotero tracker called Dos Fuegos—the two of them riding point and cut off from the others and their mounts shot from under them. Then holding flat to the ground, lying behind the mound and looking across to the rock-scrambled sand-glaring dead-silent slope where the Mimbres were. Lying unmoving—wondering if the patrol would find them.

The Mimbres came—a few at a time, running, dodging, firing carbines; and they drove them back to cover. The second rush came before they had time to reload—but so did D Company, brought by the firing, and that was that.

Sergeant Mitchell, the next month, and less talkative.

But, Mitchell thought, you really didn't learn anything that time. Not that you could apply to this one. Only that dying is important to you and if you can't do it in bed, sometime far in the future, then have it happen during a heroic act with a great number of people watching. Don't talk foolish. You're going to die, that's all . . . so do it as well as you can.

He thought of his father and mother and for a few minutes he prayed.

The woman touched his arm and he looked up. "I'm sorry . . . I wish there was something I could do."

"I wish there was too," Mitchell answered. "I wonder if you'd do me a favor."

"What is it?"

"Sometime look up my father in Banderas, R. F. Mitchell, and let him know what happened."

She nodded slowly. "All right."

Hyatt leaned forward. "Rady, your folks don't live in Banderas."

"You've got a real sense of humor," Mitchell said, mildly.

Momentarily Hyatt frowned. "You've calmed down some."

Mitchell didn't reply. He saw Dyke, standing by the big cottonwood tree, motion to the men guarding them, and now they were pulled to their feet. Hyatt turned to the woman. "Claire, we say good-bye now."

"Hy, tell them who he is."

Hyatt grinned. "Honey, I did."

"I think I'm glad they're hanging you," she said.

Hyatt shrugged. One of the possemen took Mitchell's arm. He looked at the woman and their eyes held lingeringly. Come on, he thought. You couldn't say it in minutes, so don't say it at all. He turned and followed Hyatt across the clearing and he knew that the woman was watching him.

"Get 'em up," Dyke ordered.

* * *

THEY WERE LIFTED onto the horses and a mounted man rode between them and adjusted the riata loops over their heads. Dyke looked up at them. "Mr. Rady seems to've lost his fight."

Hyatt grinned. "He's turned honest."

Mitchell looked at him. "You proved your point. Now you're wearing it out."

Hyatt's eyes narrowed. For a moment he was silent and he watched Mitchell curiously. "You ever see a hanging?" he asked then.

Mitchell shook his head. "No."

"If your neck don't bust, you strangle awhile." His eyes stayed on Mitchell. "You scared?"

Mitchell shrugged. "Probably, the same as you are."

A bewildered look crossed Hyatt's face. Apparently he had expected Mitchell to panic now, to lose control of himself pleading for his life, but he was at ease and he sat the sorrel without moving. He leaned closer so that only Mitchell could hear him say, "Rady's ten miles away by now; but in another minute he'll be legally, officially dead."

"I'd say I was doing him some favor," Mitchell answered.

Hyatt hesitated, and the cloud of uncertainty clouded his face again. He wanted to whisper, but his voice rasped. "You're going to *hang*! You understand that? Hang!"

Mitchell nodded. "The same as you are."

Hyatt's teeth clenched. He was about to say more, but he stopped.

Mitchell looked down at Dyke. "He's going to foam at the mouth in a minute."

Dyke shook his head. "He don't have that long."

But now Hyatt was looking at Mitchell calmly, without bewilderment, and without the brooding anger that had been a knife edge inside of him since the fight. That had started to die as they sat by the wagon. He had tried to bring it back by taunting Mitchell, but it was no use. His anger was dead and even the memory of it seemed senseless and unimportant. Mitchell was a man. Give him credit for it.

That's how it happened. That's what caused Hyatt to say, unexpectedly, "Reach in the side of my boot; the right one."

Dyke looked at him. "What for?"

"Just do it!"

Hyatt's eyes returned to Mitchell. "You either

got more guts than any man I ever saw . . . or else you're the dumbest."

Dyke's two fingers came out of the boot lifting the folded sheet of paper. He unfolded it and his eyes went over it slowly.

The two granite-faced men, at the very gates of a hot and waiting hell, stared stonily down at the executioner.

Dyke read it completely: the formal phrasing of the discharge order, the written-in-ink portion that described the soldier, and the scrawled, illegible signature at the bottom. He looked at the date again. Then, and only then, did he look at Mitchell.

Their eyes met briefly before Dyke turned away. He said to the men near him, "Take him down and untie him," and started toward the edge of the trees, walking with his head down. He stopped then and turned. "Hyatt Earl too. We're taking him to Mojave."

When his hands were cut loose, Mitchell walked over to Dyke. "Can I have my order now?"

Dyke handed it to him. "Listen, if I tried to tell you I'm sorry—"

Mitchell turned away. Don't listen to that, he thought. You might hit him. Don't even think of Hyatt. He looked over at the woman and saw her watching him. Then stopped. He'd have plenty of time to talk to her. And he thought, feeling the relief, but still holding himself calm: You've carried it this far. Hang on one more minute.

He turned back to Dyke and said, "Don't take it so hard, we all make mistakes."

5

The Rancher's Lady

THEY CAME TO Anton Chico on the morning stage, Willis Calender and his son, Jim; the man getting out of the coach first, stretching the stiffness from his back and squaring the curled-brim hat lower over his eyes, and then the boy, hesitating, squinting, rubbing his eyes before jumping down to stand close to his dad. It had been a long, all-night trip from the Puerto de Luna station and a six-hour ride in the wagon before that up from the Calender place in the Yeso Creek country.

Willis Calender had come to Anton Chico to marry a woman he'd never met except in letters. Three letters from him—the first two to get acquainted, the third to ask her to be his wife. She'd answered all of them, saying, yes, she was interested in the marriage state and finally she thought living down on the Yeso would be just fine. Which was exactly what the marriage broker said she would say. Her name was Clare Conway and she was to come over from Tascosa and meet Willis.

He brought Jim along because Jim was eleven, old enough to make the trip without squirming and wanting to stop every second mile, and because he was anxious for Jim to meet this woman before she became his mother. Then, the trip back to Yeso Creek would give the boy time to get used to her. Just bringing her home suddenly and saying, well, Jim, here's your new ma walking in the door, would be expecting too much of the boy; like asking him to pretend everything was still the same. Jim had been good friends with his mother—though he didn't cry at the funeral with all the people around—and he had a picture of her in his mind as fresh as yesterday. Willis Calender knew it, and this was the only thing about remarrying that bothered him.

Little Molly was different. Molly was three when her mother died, and Willis wasn't sure if the little girl even remembered her still. The first few days with the new mother might be difficult, but it would only be a matter of time. It didn't require the

kind of getting used to her that it did with Jim; so
Molly had been left home with their three-mile-
away neighbors, the Granbys. Molly was four now,
though, and she needed a mother. She was the main
reason Willis Calender had written to the Santa Fe
marriage broker, who was said to have the confi-
dence of every eligible woman from the Panhandle
to the Sangre de Cristos.

The boy looked about the early-morning street
and then to his dad, who was raising his arms to
take the mail sack the driver was lowering. He saw
the dark suit coat strain across the shoulders and
half expected to hear it rip but hoped it wouldn't,
because it was his father's only coat that made up a
suit. Usually it was hanging with mothballs in the
pockets because cattle aren't fussy about how a
man looks. It was funny to see his dad wearing it.
When was the last time? Then he remembered the
bright, silent afternoon of the funeral.

Maybe she won't be here, the boy thought,
watching the driver come down off the wheel and
take the mail sack and go up the steps of the ex-
press office. A man in range clothes was standing
there against a post, and as the boy looked that
way, their eyes met. The man said, "Hello, Jimmy,"
his mouth forming a funny half-smile in the beard
stubble that covered his mouth and jaw.

As Calender looked up, surprise seemed to sadden his weathered face. He put his big hand behind the boy's shoulder and moved him forward toward the steps and said, "Hello, Dick." Only that.

Dick Maddox was still against the post, his thumbs crooked in his belt. Another man in range clothes was on the other side of the post from him. Maddox nodded and said, "Will." Then added, "I'm surprised you brought your boy along."

"Why would that be?" Calender said.

"Well, it ain't many boys see their dad get married."

"How'd you know about that?"

"Things get around," Maddox said easily. "You know, I was surprised Clare didn't ask one of us fellas to give her away."

★　★　★

CALENDER LOOKED at the man steadily, trying to hide his surprise, and hesitated so it wouldn't show in his voice. "You know Miss Conway?"

Maddox glanced at the man next to him. "He says do I know *Miss* Conway." Both of them grinned. "Well, I'd say anybody who's followed the Canadian to Tascosa knows *Miss* Conway, and that's just about everybody."

The words came like a slap in the face, but Calender thought: Hold on to yourself. And he kept his voice natural when he said, "What do you mean by that?"

Maddox straightened slightly against the post. "You're marrying her, you must've known she worked at the Casa Grande."

Calender was suddenly conscious of his boy looking up at him. He said, "Come on, Jim." And, glancing at Dick Maddox: "We've got to move along."

They started up the street toward the two-story hotel, and Maddox called, "What time's the wedding?" The man with him laughed. Calender heard them but he didn't look around.

When they were farther up the street, the boy said, "Who was that man?"

"Maddox is his name," Calender said. "He used to be old man Granby's herd boss. Now I guess he works around here."

They were silent, and then the boy said, "Why'd you get mad when he started talking about *her*?"

"Who got mad?"

"Well, it looked like it."

"Most of the time that man doesn't know what he's talking about," Will Calender said. "Maybe I looked mad because I had to stand there and be civil while he wasted air."

"All he said was other people knew her," the boy said.

"All right, let's not talk about it any more."

"I didn't see anything wrong in that."

Calender didn't answer.

"Maybe he was good friends with her."

Calender turned on the boy suddenly, but his judgment held him, and after a moment he spoke quietly: "I said let's not talk about it any more."

But it stayed in his mind, and now there was an urgency inside him, an impatience to meet this woman face to face and try to read there what her past had been. It was strange. From the letters he had never doubted she was anything but a good woman, but now— And with this uncertainty the fear began to grow, the fear that he'd see something on her face, some mark of an easy woman.

Damn Maddox! Why'd he have to say it in front of the boy! But he could be just talking, insinuating what isn't so, Calender thought. A man like that ought to have his tongue cut out. All he's good for is drink and talk. Ask old man Granby, he got his bellyful of Maddox and fired him.

They went into the hotel, into the quiet, dim lobby with its high-beamed ceiling. Their eyes lifted to the second-floor balcony which extended all the way around, except for the front side, so that all of the hotel's eleven rooms looked down on the lobby, where, around the balcony support posts, were cane-bottom Douglas chairs and cuspidors and here and there parts of newspapers. The room was empty, except for the man behind the desk who watched them indifferently. His hair glistened flat on an angle over his forehead, and a matchstick barely showed in the corner of his mouth.

"Miss Conway," Will Calender said. The name was loud in the highceilinged room, and he felt embarrassed hearing himself say it.

"You're Mr. Calender?"

"That's right." Calender thought: How does he know my name? He stared at the room clerk closely. If he starts to grin, I'll hit him.

"Miss Conway is in number five." The clerk nodded vaguely up the balcony.

Calender hesitated. "Would she be—up yet?"

The clerk started to grin, and Calender thought: Watch yourself, boy. But the clerk just said, "Why don't you go up and knock on the door?"

The boy frowned, watching his father climb the stairs and move along the balcony. He was walking funny, like his feet hurt. Maybe she won't be there, the boy thought hopefully. Maybe she changed her mind. No, she'll be there. He pictured her coming down the stairs, then smiling and patting his cheek

and saying, "So this is *Jimmy*." A smile that would
be gone and suddenly come back again. "My, but
Jimmy is a fine-looking young man. How old are
you, Jimmy?" She'll be fat and smelly like Mrs.
Granby and those other ladies down on Yeso Creek.
How come all women get so fat? All except Ma.
She wasn't fat and she smelled nice and she never
called me Jimmy. He felt a funny feeling remembering his mother, the sound of her voice and the easy
way she did things without complaining or getting
excited. What did Molly have to have a mother for?
She's gotten along for a year without one.

He saw the door open, but caught only a glimpse
of the woman. His father went inside then, but the
door remained open.

The room clerk grinned and winked at the boy.
"Now, if that was me, I think I'd close the door."

A moment later they came out of the room. The
boy watched his father close the door and follow
the woman along the balcony to the stairs and then
down. The woman was younger than he'd imagined
her, much younger, with a funny hat and blond hair
fixed in a bun. And she wasn't fat; if anything,
skinny. Her face was slender, the skin pale-clear
and her eyes seemed sad. The boy looked at her until she got close.

"This here is my son," Will Calender said. "We

left Molly at the Granbys'. She's only four years old"—he smiled self-consciously—"like I told you in the letters."

The woman smiled back at him. She seemed ill at ease but she said, "How do you do?" to the boy, and her voice was calm and without the false enthusiasm of Will Calender's.

The boy said, "Ma'am," not looking at her face now but noticing her slender white hands holding the ends of the crocheted shawl in front of her.

A silence followed, and Will Calender suggested that they could get something to eat. He had intended mentioning Maddox's name up in the room then watch her reaction, but there hadn't been time. She didn't look like the kind Maddox hinted she was, did she? Maybe Maddox was just talking. She was better-looking than he'd expected. Those eyes and that low, calm voice. Dick Maddox better watch his mouth.

They went to the café next door for breakfast. Calender and the boy ordered eggs and meat, but Clare Conway just took coffee, because she wasn't very hungry. Most of the time they ate in silence. Every now and then Will Calender could hear himself chewing and he'd move his fork on the plate or stir at his coffee with the spoon scraping the bottom of the cup. Clare said the coffee was very good. And, maybe a minute later: It's going to be a nice day. It's so dry out here you can stand the extra heat.

Then it was Will's turn. Where you from originally? . . . New Orleans. . . . I never been there but I hear it's a nice town. . . . It's all right. . . . Silence. . . . How long'd you live in Tascosa? . . . Five years. My husband was with one of the cattle companies. . . . Oh. . . . He died three years ago. . . . Silence. . . . That's right, you told me in your letter. . . . That's right, I did. . . . Silence. . . . What've you been doing since then? . . . I took a position. . . . Calender's jaw was set. . . . At the Casa Grande? . . . Clare Conway blushed suddenly. She nodded and took a sip of coffee in the silence.

There were two men at a table near them and Will Calender had the feeling one nudged the other, and they both grinned, looking over, then looked away quickly when Calender shot a glance toward them.

Calender passed the back of his hand across his mouth and cleared his throat. "Miss Conway, I planned on ordering some stores this morning, long as I was here. They're hauled down to Puerto de Luna, and I pick 'em up there. Some seed and flour"—he cleared his throat again—"and I have to speak to the justice yet." He looked quickly toward the front window, though it wasn't necessary because Clare's eyes were on her coffee cup.

"Jim, here, will stay with you." The boy looked at him with a plea in his eyes, and Will scowled. Then he rose and walked out without looking at the woman.

Standing in front of the hotel, Dick Maddox looked over toward the café as Calender came out, putting on his hat. Maddox glanced at the three men with him, and they grinned as he looked back toward Calender, who was coming toward them now.

"You married yet, Will?"

Calender glanced at Maddox's closed face, at the beard bristles and the cigarette and the eyes in the shadow of the hat brim. "Not yet," he said, and looked straight ahead again, not slowing his stride.

Maddox waited until he was looking at Calender's back. He drew on the cigarette and exhaled and said slowly, "Some men will marry just about anything."

Calender's boots sounded on the planking one, two, three, then stopped. He came around. "Do you mean me, Dick?"

* * *

A SMILE TOUCHED the corner of Dick Maddox's mouth. "Old man Granby used to have a saying: If the shoe fits, wear it."

"You can talk plainer than that."

"How plain, Will?"

"Talk like a man for a change."

"Well, as a man, I'm wondering if you're going to go ahead and marry this—*Miss* Conway." One of the men behind him laughed but cut it off.

"What if I am?"

Maddox shrugged. "Every man to his own taste."

Calender stepped closer to him. "Dick, if I was married to that woman and you said what you have—you'd be dead right now."

"That's opinion, Will." Maddox smiled because he was sure he could take Will Calender and he wanted to make sure the three men with him knew it.

Calender said, "The point is, I'm not married to her yet. Not yet. If you don't come out with what's on your mind now, you better not come out with it about two hours from now."

Maddox shook his head. "You're a warnin' man, Will."

"What did she do in Tascosa?" Calender said bluntly.

Maddox hesitated, grinning. "Worked at the Casa Grande."

"And that's what?"

"You never been to Tascosa?"

"I just never saw the place."

"Well, the Casa Grande's where a sweaty trail hand goes for his drink, gamblin', and girls." Maddox paused. "I could draw you a picture, Will."

"Dick, if you're pullin' a joke—"

"Ask anybody in town."

Calender looked at the hat-brim shadow and the eyes, the eyes that held without wavering. Then he turned and went up the street.

From his office window, Hillpiper, the Anton Chico Justice of the Peace, watched Will Calender cross the street. The office was above the jail and offered a view of sun, dust, and adobe; there was nothing else to see in Anton Chico, unless you were looking down the streets east, then you'd see the Pecos.

Hillpiper sat down at his desk, hearing the boots on the stairs, and when the knock came he said, "Come in, Will."

"How'd you know it was me?"

"Sit down." Hillpiper smiled. "You had an appointment for this morning, and I've got a window." Hillpiper wore silver-rim spectacles for close work, but he looked over them to Calender sitting across the desk from him.

Calender said, "You know what everybody in town's saying?"

Hillpiper shook his head. "Not everybody."

"They're talking about this woman I'm to marry."

"I'll say it again. Not everybody."

Calender's raw-boned face was tightening, and his voice was louder. "How can they know so much about her—and me, the man that's to marry her, not know anything?"

"It's happened before," Hillpiper said.

"You heard what they're saying?"

"I heard Maddox in the saloon last night. Is he the everybody you're talking about?"

"He's enough. But it's what she is!" Calender said savagely. "What she didn't tell in her letters!"

"Three letters," Hillpiper said mildly. Calender had told him about it when he made the arrangements and set the date: the marriage broker in Santa Fe writing to him, then writing to the woman. Hillpiper had told him it was all right as far as he was concerned, since he didn't see why two people had to love each other to get along. Love's something that might come, but if it didn't— look at all the marriages getting on without it. And Calender had said, That's right. I never thought of that. See, my little girl's the main reason.

"In three letters," Hillpiper went on, "a woman hardly has time to open up her heart."

"She could have told me what she did!"

"Just what does she do, Will?"

"You heard Maddox."

"I want to hear it from you."

"She worked at the Casa Grande!" Calender flared. "How do you want me to say it?"

Hillpiper put his palms on the desk and leaned forward. "All right, Will, she worked in a saloon. She danced with trail hands, maybe sang a little and smiled more than was natural to get the boys to buy the extra drink they'd a bought anyway. And that's all she's done, regardless of how Maddox makes a dozen words sound like a whole story. Why she did that kind of work, I don't know. Maybe she had to because there was nothing else for a girl to do and she still had to eat like anybody else. Maybe it killed her to do it. Or"—Hillpiper's voice was quieter and he shrugged—"maybe she liked doing it. Maybe she forgot where she carried her morals—assuming what she was doing is morally wrong. By most men's standards it is wrong for a female to work in a saloon, your standards too or you wouldn't be here with your face tied in a knot. But those same men have a hell of a good time with the females when they're at the Casa Grande."

Hillpiper smiled faintly. "You were always a little

stricter than most men anyway, Will. Seems like most of your life you've been a hard-working, Bible-reading family man, with no time for places like the Casa Grande. You've sweated your ranch into something pretty nice, something most other men wouldn't have the patience or the guts to do. And I can see you not wanting to chance ruining all you've built—ranch or family. That's why I was a little surprised when you of all people came in with this mail-order romance idea. I suspect, now that I think about it, you had the idea if a girl wants to get married she's the simon-pure family type and nothing else. You had a good woman before, Will; so you expected one just as good this time."

Hillpiper leaned a little closer, his eyes on Calender's weathered face. "Will," Hillpiper said. "You might be shocked a little bit, but when you get to heaven you're going to see a lot of faces you never expected to see. Folks who got up there on God's standards and not man's. For all you know, you're liable to even see Dick Maddox—though I suppose that would be stretching divine mercy a little thin."

Anton Chico's Justice of the Peace leaned back in his swivel chair, his coat opening to show a gold watch chain across his vest. His hand came out of a side pocket with a cigar, and with a match from a vest pocket he lit it, puffing a cloud of smoke. When he looked up, Calender was standing.

"What've you decided, Will?"

"I've got my kids to think about."

"It's your problem." Hillpiper said this in a kindly way, stating a fact. "If you've decided not to go through with it, that's your business."

Will Calender nodded. "I suppose I should pay her stage fare back to Tascosa."

"That would be nice, Will," Hillpiper said mildly.

Calender thanked him and went out, down the stairs and into the street. Crossing to the other side, he felt awkward and self-conscious. The suit coat held tight across the shoulders and he could feel his big hands hanging too far out of the sleeves, and with nothing to hold on to.

It's gotten hot, he thought, pulling his hat lower. Maybe the dryness makes it easier on some people, but it's still hot. And then he thought: I'd better tell her before I buy the stage ticket.

☆ ☆ ☆

DICK MADDOX was still in front of the hotel, but now more men were there. It had gotten around that Maddox was having some fun with Will Calender, so they drifted over casually from here and

there, the ones who knew Maddox standing closest
to him, laughing at what he said. The rest were all
along the hotel's shady ramada. One of the men
saw Calender coming and he nudged Maddox, who
looked up, then pretended he wasn't concerned, until Calender was close to the hotel entrance.

"You change your mind, Will?"

Calender stopped and breathed out wearily, "If
you showed as much concern for your own business, you'd be a well-to-do man."

"You can't take kiddin', can you?"

"Why should I have to?"

"You got a lot to learn, Will."

Calender shrugged, because he was tired of this,
and went inside.

The boy was sitting alone, with his heels hooked
in the wooden rungs of the chair. When he saw his
father he jumped up quickly.

Calender looked about to be certain the woman
was not in the lobby.

"Where is she?" he asked the boy.

"She went upstairs. All of a sudden she just
started crying and went upstairs."

"What?"

"It was when they started talking. We were sitting here, and then her chin started to shake—you
know—and then she run upstairs."

"Who was talking? The men outside?" The boy nodded hurriedly, and Calender could see that he was frightened and trying to hide it and at the same time was not sure what it was all about.

"What did they say?"

"Just one of them, the rest were laughing most of the time. He was telling them"—the boy said it slowly as if he'd memorized it—"he said some women didn't know their place. They think they can live in the gutter then go out when they want and brush against people like nothing's coming off. He was talking loud so we could hear every word and he said a man would be a fool to marry a woman like that and have her brushing against his kids with her gutter ways. It was like that, what he said. Then he spoke your name and he said he'd bet anybody five dollars American you'd changed your mind now about getting married. That's when she run upstairs."

The boy frowned, looking at his father, watching his eyes go up to the room. "Why'd he have to say things like that? We were sitting here talking— getting acquainted."

Calender looked at the boy and saw that he was grinning.

"You know she never once asked me how old I was or if I knew my reader or things like that. She talked to me about affairs and interesting things like I was grown up, like Ma used to do. And, Pa, she called me *Jim*! Can you imagine that? She called me *Jim*! If her hair was darker and her nose a little different, I'd swear she was Ma!"

"Don't say things like that!" Calender was conscious of his voice, and he said quietly, "There's the difference of night and day."

"Well, her voice is different too, and maybe she's a speck taller, though that could be the hat. I never seen Ma in a regular hat. But outside of that, they sure are alike."

"You know what you're saying, comparing this woman with your mother?"

The boy looked at him questioningly, but the trace of a smile was still on his face. "I'm just saying they're alike, that's all. Maybe they don't look so much alike, but they sure are alike." The boy smiled; he was sure his explanation was clear because he understood it so well himself.

Calender was looking at the boy closely now. "What if she's done something bad?"

"Pa, little Molly's doing bad things all the time. That's just the way girls are. Most times they're not doing serious things, so they have more time to get theirselves into trouble."

Calender's eyes remained on the boy. Calender asked: "You think Molly will like her?"

"Couple of bad women like them will get along just fine." The boy grinned.

Calender left him abruptly, going up the stairs. In a few minutes he came back down, and in front of him was Clare Conway.

They walked across the lobby. Nearing the door, the woman hesitated and looked up at Will Calender. She was unsure and afraid. It was in her wide-open eyes, in the way her fingers held the ends of the crocheted shawl. Then she moved on again as if not under her own power—when Will touched her elbow and said to the boy, "Come on, Jim."

And when they were out on the ramada the woman's eyes were looking down at her hands; she could feel Will Calender holding her elbow, she could feel the guiding pressure of his hand, and moved to the right along the ramada, along the line of silent men, hearing only her footsteps and the footsteps of the man at her side. The hand on her elbow tightened. She was being turned gently, and there was no longer the sound of footsteps and when she looked up a man was close in front of her, a man with heavy beard bristles.

"Miss Conway," Calender said. "This is Mr.

Maddox. He's had such a keen interest in our business, I thought you might like to meet him."

"Now, Will—" Maddox said, looking at Calender strangely.

"And, Dick," Calender went on, "this is Miss Conway. Isn't there something you wanted to say to her?"

"Will—"

"Maybe you'd just like to tip your hat like a gentleman."

Maddox was staring at Calender almost dumbfounded, but slowly his face relaxed as he realized what Calender was doing in front of all these men and he said mildly, grinning, "Now, Will, I don't know if I want to do that or not."

Calender's fist came around suddenly, unexpectedly, driving against Maddox's jaw, changing the smile to lopsided surprise and sending him back off the ramada into the street. Calender followed, and hit him again and this time Maddox went down, his hat falling off in front of him. Maddox started to rise, but Calender came for him again. Maddox hesitated, then eased down and sat in the street, looking up at Calender.

"One other thing, Dick," Will said. "I hear you're taking bets there isn't going to be a wedding today." He glanced back at the crowd of men in the shade. "Who's holding the stakes?"

There was a silence, then someone called, "Nobody'd bet him."

Calender beckoned to the man. "Come here." He brought a five-dollar gold piece out of his pants pocket and gave it to the man. "Dick Maddox'll give you one just like this. Now you add the two up and have that much ready for me when I get back."

He walked to the ramada. The tension was gone. Some of the men were whispering and talking, some just looking out at Maddox still sitting in the street.

The boy's face was beaming as he watched his father. Clare came toward him.

"You ripped the seam of your coat up the back," she said.

He felt her hand on his back pulling the cloth together. "Gives me a little more room," he said, conscious of the men watching him.

"It's your good coat, though," the woman said. "I'll mend it soon as we get home."

6

Moment of Vengeance

AT MIDMORNING six riders came down out of the cavernous pine shadows, down the slope swept yellow with arrowroot blossoms, down through the scattered aspen at the north end of the meadow, then across the meadow and into the yard of the one-story adobe house.

Four of the riders dismounted, three of these separating as they moved toward the house; the fourth took his rope and walked off toward the mesquite-pole corral. The horses in the enclosure stood and watched as he opened the gate.

Ivan Kergosen, still mounted, motioned to the open stable shed that was built out from the adobe.

The sixth man rode up to it, looked inside, then continued around the corner and was out of sight.

Now Kergosen, tight-jawed and solemn, saw the door of the adobe open. He watched Ellis, his daughter, come out to the edge of the ramada shade, ignoring the three men, who stepped aside to let her pass.

"We've been expecting you," she said. Her voice was calm and her smile, for a moment, seemed genuine, but it faded too quickly. She touched her dark hair, smoothing it as a breeze rose and swept across the yard.

"Where is he?" Kergosen said.

Her gaze lifted, going out across the open sunlight of the meadow to the far west corner, to the windmill that stood out faintly against a dark background of pines.

"He's at the stock tank," Ellis said. "But he'll come in now."

Mr. Kergosen's hands were gripped one over the other on the saddle horn. He stared at his daughter in silence, his mustache hiding his mouth, but not the iron-willed anger in his eyes and in the tight line of his jaw.

"Whether he does or not," Kergosen said, "you're going back with me."

"I'm married now, Pa."

"Don't talk foolish."

"Married in Willson. By a priest."

"We'll talk about that at home."

"I am home!"

"Girl, this isn't going to be a public debate."

"Then why did you bring an audience?" She was sorry as soon as she said it. "Pa, I don't mean disrespect. Phil and I were married in Willson five days ago. He bought stock, drove it here, and we intend to raise it." Her father stared at her, saying nothing, and to fill the silence she added, "This is my home now, where I've come to live with my husband."

Leo Pyke, one of the three men standing near her, the curled brim of his hat straight and low over his eyes, said, "Looks more like a wickiup. Someplace a 'Pache would bring his squaw." He grinned, leaning against a support post, staring at Ellis.

Mr. Kergosen did not look up, but said, "Shut up, Leo."

"It's no fit place," Pyke said, straightening. "That's all I'm saying."

"Phil has work to do on it," Ellis said defensively. "He's already put on a new roof." She looked quickly at her father. "That's what I mean. We didn't just run off and get married. We've planned for it. Phil paid down on the house and property more than a month ago at the Dos Mesas bank. Since then we've be making it livable."

"Behind my back," Kergosen said.

Ellis hesitated. "Phil wanted to ask your permission. I told him it wouldn't do any good."

"How did you suppose that?" her father asked.

"I've lived with you for eighteen years, Pa. I know you."

"Can you say you know Phil Treat as well?"

"I know him," Ellis said simply.

"As far as I'm concerned," Kergosen said, "he qualifies as a man. But certainly not as the man who marries my daughter."

Ellis asked, "And I have nothing to say about it?"

"We're not discussing it here," Kergosen said.

He had hired Treat almost a year ago, during the time he was having trouble with the San Carlos Reservation people. He lost two men that spring and roughly two dozen head of beef to raiding parties. The Apache police did nothing about it, though they knew his stock was being taken to San Carlos. So Ivan Kergosen went to Fort Thomas and hired a professional tracker whose government contract had expired, and went after them himself. They turned out to be Chiricahuas and the scout ran down every last one of them.

The scout's name was Phil Treat. He had been a

soldier, buffalo hunter, and cavalry guide, and had earned a reputation as a gunfighter by killing three men: two of them at Tascosa when they tried to steal his hides; the third one at Anton Chico, New Mexico—an Army deserter who drew his gun, refusing to go back to Apache land. Only three, but the shootings were done well, with witnesses, and it took no more than that to establish a reputation.

And after the trouble was past, Phil Treat stayed on with Mr. Kergosen. He was passing fair with cattle, a good horsebreaker, and an A-1 hunter; so Kergosen paid him top wages and was pleased to have such a man around. But as a hired hand; not as a son-in-law.

All his life Ivan Kergosen had worked hard and prayed hard, asking God for guidance. He built his holdings according to a single-minded interpretation of God's will, respecting Him more as a God of Justice than a God of Mercy. And his good fortune, he believed, was God in His justice rewarding him, granting him success in life for adhering to Divine Will. It had taken Ivan Kergosen thirty years of working and fighting—fighting the land, the Apache, and anyone who tried to take from his land—to build the finest spread in the Pinaleño Valley. He built this success for his own self-respect, for his wife who was now deceased, and for his daughter, Ellis—not for a sign-reading gunfighter who'd spent half of his life killing buffalo, the other tracking Apache, and who now, somehow, contrary to all his plans, had married his daughter.

He heard Leo Pyke's voice and he was brought back to the here and now. "Fixing the house while he was working for you, Mr. Kergosen," Pyke was saying. "No telling the amount of sneaky acts he's committed."

The man who had gone to the corral came out, leading a saddled and bridled dun horse. He looked back over his shoulder, then at Mr. Kergosen, and called, "He's coming now!"

Ellis was aware then of the steady cantering sound. She saw Leo Pyke and the two men with him—Sandal, who was a Mexican, and Grady, a bearded, solemn-faced man—look out past the corral, and she said, "In a moment you can say it to his face, Leo. About being sneaky."

She looked up in time to see her husband swing past the corral, coming toward her. She watched him dismount stiffly. He let the reins drop, passed his hand over his mouth, then up to his hat brim, and loosened it from his forehead. He turned his back to the three men in the ramada shade as if intentionally ignoring them; then looked from Ellis to her father and said, "Well?"

And now Ivan Kergosen was faced with the calm, deliberate gaze of this man. He saw that Phil Treat was not wearing a gun; he saw that he was trail dirty and had moved slowly, to stand now, tall but stooped, with his hands hanging empty.

He could handle this man. Kergosen was sure of that now, but he respected him and he had planned this meeting carefully. Leo Pyke, who openly disliked Treat, and Sandal and Grady, who had been with him longer than any of his other riders, would deal with Treat if he objected. No, there would be no trouble. But he formed his words carefully before he spoke.

Then he said, "You made a mistake. So did my daughter. But both mistakes are corrected as of this moment. Ellis is going home and you have ten minutes to pack your gear and get out. Clear?"

"And my stock?" Treat said.

"You're selling your stock to me," Kergosen said, "so there' be nothing to delay you." His hand went into his coat and came out with a folded square of green paper. "My draft on the Willson Bank to cover the sale of your yearling stock. Thirty head. When you draw the money, the canceled draft is my receipt." He extended his hand. "Take it." Treat did not move and Kergosen's wrist flicked out and the folded paper floated—fell to the ground. "Pick

it up," Kergosen said. "Your time's running out."
He looked at Ellis then. "Mount up."

★ ★ ★

ELLIS ALMOST SPOKE, frightened, angry, and unsure of herself now, but she looked at her husband
and waited.

Treat stood motionless, still gazing up at Kergosen. "You have five men and I have myself," he
said. "That makes a difference, doesn't it?"

"If this is unjust," Kergosen said, "then it's unjust.
I'll say it only once more. Your time's running out."

Treat's eyes moved to Ellis. "Do what he says."
He saw the bewildered look come over her face,
and he said, "Go home with him, Ellis, and do
what he tells you." Treat paused. "But don't speak
one solitary word to him as long as you're under his
roof. Not till I come for you." He said this quietly
in the brittle silence that hung over the yard, and
now he saw Ellis nod her head slowly.

He looked up at Kergosen, who was staring at
him intently. "Mr. Kergosen, we can't argue with
you and we can't fight you, but take Ellis home and
you'll know she isn't just your daughter anymore."

"You don't threaten me," Kergosen said.

"No," Treat said, "you've got iron fists, a hundred and thirty square miles of land, and you sit

there like it's the high seat of judgment. But you live with Ellis now, if you can."

Kergosen said, "Pick up that draft."

Treat shook his head.

"As God is my judge, I mean you no harm," Kergosen said. "But you don't leave me a choice."

He nodded to Leo Pyke as he reined his bay in a tight circle and rode out. Ellis had mounted and now she followed him, looking back past the two riders who fell in behind her as she passed the corral and started across the meadow.

They were not yet out of sight, but nearing the aspen stands when Pyke said to Sandal and Grady, "So he won't pick it up."

Treat looked at him, then stooped, without loss of dignity, unhurriedly, and picked up the draft. "If it bothers you," he said.

Pyke grinned. "He's not so big now, is he?"

The Mexican rider, Sandal, said, "Like a field hand. I thought he was something with a gun."

"A story he made up," the third man, Grady, said.

Pyke said to Sandal, "Move his horse out of the way."

Sandal winked at Grady. "And the Henry, uh?" He led Treat's claybank to the corral and lifted the Henry rifle from the saddle boot as he shooed him in. He walked back to them, studying the rifle, holding it at belt level. Without looking at them, as if not aiming, he flipped the lever down and up and fired past them, and the right front window of the adobe shattered.

Sandal looked up, smiling. "This is no bad gun."

Across the meadow two of Kergosen's riders were moving the herd away from the stock tank. Treat watched them, turning his back to Sandal. There was time. These men would do as they pleased, whether he objected or not. Wait and say nothing, he thought. Wait and watch and keep track of the score.

He remembered a patrol out of Fort Thomas coming to a spring, and a Coyotero Apache guide whose name was Pesh-klitso. The guide had said to him in Spanish, "We followed the barbarian for ten days; two men died, three horses died; we have no food and we killed no barbarian. Yet we could have waited for them here. Our stomachs would be full, the two men and the horses would still be alive, and we would take them when they came." He'd asked the Coyotero how he knew they would come, and the guide answered, "The land is not that broad. They would come sooner or later." Which meant, if not today, then tomorrow; if not this year, then the next.

He had known many Pesh-klitsos at San Carlos,

and at Tascosa, when they carried Sharps rifles and hunted buffalo—hunted them by waiting, then killed them. And the more patience you had the more you killed.

Treat waited and watched. He watched Grady go into the adobe and saw the left front window erupt with a spray of broken glass as a chair came through. He saw Sandal break off two of the chair legs with the heel of his boot, then walk into the adobe, and a moment later the Henry was firing again. With the reports, the ear-ringing din and the clicking cocking sound of the lever, he heard glass and china shattering, falling from the shelves. Then the sound of a Colt and a dull, clanging noise; sooty smoke billowed from the open doorway and he knew they had shot down the stove chimney.

Grady came out, fanning the smoke in front of him. He mounted his horse, sidestepped it to the ramada, fastened the loop of his rope to a support post, and spurred away. The post ripped out, bouncing, scraping a dust rise, and the mesquite-pole awning sagged partway to the ground. Sandal came out of the adobe, running, ducking his head. He watched Grady circle to come back, went to his own horse, fastened his rope to the other support post, and dragged it away. The ramada collapsed, swinging, smashing, against the adobe front, and the mesquite poles broke apart.

Watching Treat, Leo Pyke said, "You letting them get away with that? All this big talk about you, and you don't even open your mouth."

Grady and Sandal walked their horses in. Treat glanced at them, then back to Pyke. "I don't have anything to say."

"Listen," Pyke said. "I've put up with that close-mouth cold-water way of yours a long time. I've watched men stand clear of you, afraid they'd step too close and you'd come to life. I watched Mr. Kergosen, then Ellis, won over to your sly ways. But all that time I was seeing through you—looking clean through, and there was nothing there to see. No backbone, no guts, no nothing."

Sandal was grinning, leaning over his saddle horse. "Eat him up, Layo!"

Pyke's eyes did not leave Treat. "If you were worth it, I'd take my gun off and beat hell out of you."

Treat's eyebrows raised slightly. "Would you, Leo?"

"You damn bet I would."

Sandal said, "Go ahead, man. Do it."

"Shut your mouth!" Pyke threw the words over his shoulder.

"The vision of being segundo returns with the return of the daughter," Sandal said, grinning again.
To Grady, next to him, he said, "How would you
like to work for this one every day?"

Grady shook his head. "She can't marry him
now. And that's the only way he'd get to be Number Two."

"I think she married him," Sandal said, nodding
at Treat, "to escape this one."

"I said shut up!" Pyke screamed, turning half
around, but at once he looked back at Treat. "You
ride out, right now. And if I ever see you this close
again, I'll talk to you with a gun. You hear me!"

★ ★ ★

NINE DAYS AFTER that, R. C. Hassett, the county
deputy assigned to Dos Mesas, was told of the dis-
appearance of two of Ivan Kergosen's riders. On
Saturday, two days before, they'd spent the evening
in town. They started back home at eleven o'clock
and had not been seen since.

Hassett thought it over the length of time it took
him to strap on his holster and take a Winchester
down from the wall rack. Then he rode out to Phil
Treat's place. Entering the yard, he heard a ham-
mering sound coming from the adobe. He saw that
a new ramada had been constructed. As he reined

toward the adobe, Phil Treat stepped out of the doorway, a Henry rifle under his arm.

"So you're rebuilding," Hassett said. "I heard about what happened."

His eyes held on Treat as he stepped out of the saddle, letting his reins trail. He brushed open his coat and took a tobacco plug from his vest pocket, bit off a corner of it, and returned the plug to the pocket. His coat remained open, the skirt held back by the butt of his revolver. He had been a law officer for more than two dozen years and he was in no particular hurry.

"I wasn't sure you'd be here," said Hassett. "But something told me to find out."

"You're not looking for me," Treat said.

"No; two of Mr. Kergosen's boys."

Treat called toward the adobe, "Come out a minute!"

Hassett watched as Grady and Sandal appeared in the doorway, then came outside. Grady's bearded face was bruised, one eye swollen and half closed, and he limped as he took the few steps out to the end of the ramada shade. There was no mark on Sandal.

"These the men?" asked Treat. Hassett nodded.

"Ivan reported them lost."

"Not lost," Treat said. "They quit him to work for me."

"Without drawing their pay?"

"That's none of my business," Treat answered.

Hassett's gaze moved to the adobe. "Grady, I didn't know you were a carpenter."

The bearded man hesitated before saying, "I'm swearing out a complaint on one Phil Treat."

Hassett nodded, moving the tobacco from one cheek to the other. "It's your privilege, Grady; though I'd say you got off easy."

"This man forced us—" Grady began.

Hassett held up his hand. "In my office." He looked at Treat then. "You come in, too, and state your complaint. I make out a writ and serve it on Ivan. The writ orders him to court on such and such a date. You're there to claim your wife with proof of legal marriage."

"And if Mr. Kergosen doesn't appear?" asked Treat.

"He's no bigger than I am," Hassett said. "I see that he does next time."

"But that doesn't calm his mind, does it?"

"That's your problem," Hassett said.

Treat almost smiled. "You said it as simply as it can be said."

"All right," Hassett said. "You've been told." He moved around his horse, stepped up into the saddle, then looked down at Treat again. "Let me ask you something. How come Grady looks the way he does and there isn't a mark on Sandal?"

"I talked to Grady first," Treat said.

"I see," Hassett said. "I'll ask you something else. How come Ivan didn't come here looking for these two?"

"I guess he doesn't know I'm still here."

Hassett looked down at Treat. "But he'll know it now, won't he?" He turned and rode out of the yard.

That afternoon, after they had finished the inside repairs, Sandal and Grady were released. They rode out, riding double, and watching them, Treat pictured them approaching the great U-shaped adobe that was Mr. Kergosen's home, then dismounting and standing in the sunlight as Ivan came down the steps from the veranda.

Sandal would tell it: how they were ambushed riding back from Dos Mesas, how Treat had appeared in front of them, coming out of the trees with the Henry; how Grady's horse had been hit when they tried to run, and had fallen on Grady and injured his ankle; how they had been taken back to his adobe and forced to rebuild the ramada and patch the furniture and the stove. And Sandal would describe him as some kind of demon, a *nagual* who never slept and seldom spoke as he held them with a Henry rifle for two days and two nights.

Ivan Kergosen would turn from them, his eyes going to Ellis sitting on the shaded veranda, reading or sewing or staring out over the yard. She would not look at him, but he would detect the beginning of a smile. Only this, on the tenth day of her silence.

You have a woman, Treat thought, picturing her. *You have one and you don't have one.* He thought of the time he had first spoken to her, the times they rode together and the time he first kissed her.

And now they'll come again. But not Grady, because his ankle will put him to bed. Outwait an old man, he thought. *Wait while an old man realizes he is not God, or God's avenging angel, God's right hand. Which could take no longer than your lifetime,* he thought.

He took dried meat, a canteen, a blanket, the Henry, and a holstered Colt revolver and went out into the corral to wait for them.

★ ★ ★

THERE WERE FIVE that came. They reached Treat's adobe at dusk, spreading out as they approached it, coming at it from both sides of the corral, two of the riders circling the stable shed and the adobe before entering the yard. Sandal dismounted and went into the adobe. He came out with a kerosene lantern and held it as Pyke struck a match and lit it.

"Who's going to do it?" asked Sandal.

"You're holding the fire," Pyke said.

"Not me." Sandal shook his head.

"Just throw it in. Hit the wall over the bed."

"Not me. I've done enough to that man."

"What about what he did to you?"

"He had reason."

Pyke stepped out of the saddle. He jerked the lantern away from Sandal and walked to the door. His hand went to the latch, then stopped.

"Layo!" Sandal's voice.

Pyke looked over his shoulder, saw Sandal not looking at him, but staring out toward the corral, and he turned full around, holding the lantern by the ring handle.

He saw Treat crossing the yard toward him. In the dusk he could not see the man's features, but he knew it was Treat. He saw Treat's hands hanging empty and he saw the revolver on his right leg. Now Sandal was moving the horses, holding the reins and whack-slapping at the rump of one to force both of them to the side. The horses of the three riders still mounted moved nervously, and the riders watched Treat, seeing him looking at Leo Pyke. Then, thirty feet from the ramada, Treat stopped.

"Leo, you tore my house down once. Once is enough."

Pyke was at ease. "You're going to stop us?"

"The last time you stated that you'd talk with a gun if I ever came close again." Treat glanced at Sandal when Pyke said nothing. "Is that right?"

"Big as life," the Mexican said.

Treat's gaze returned to Pyke. "Well?"

"You got me at an unfair advantage," Pyke said carefully. "A lantern in my hand. All the light full on me."

"You came here to burn down my house," Treat said, standing motionless. "You're holding the fire, as you told Sandal. You've four men backing you and you call it a disadvantage."

"Three men backing him," Sandal said.

Beyond him one of the mounted riders said, "This part of it isn't our fight."

And Sandal added, "Just Layo's."

"Wait a minute." Pyke was taken by surprise. "You all work for Mr. Kergosen. He says run him out, we do it!"

"But not carry him out," the one who had spoken before said. "You threatened him, Leo; then it's your fight, not ours. And if you think he's got an unfair advantage, put the lantern down."

"So it's like that," Pyke said.

"You got two feet," Sandal said. "Stand on them. Show us how the segundo would do it."

"Listen, you chili picker! You're through!"

"Sure, Layo. Now talk to that boy out there."

"Mr. Kergosen's going to run every damn one of you!" Pyke half turned to face them, shifting the lantern to his left hand, the light swaying across Sandal and the chestnut color of his horse.

"We'll talk to him," Sandal said.

Pyke stared at him. "You know what you done, you and the rest? You jawed yourself out of jobs. You see how easy a new one is to find. Mr. Kergosen's going to be burned, but sure as hell I'm going to"—his feet started to shift—"tell him!"

As he said it, Pyke was spinning on his toes, swinging the lantern hard at Treat, seeing it in the air, then going to his right, but seeing Treat moving, with the revolver suddenly in his hand, and at that moment Treat fired.

Pyke was half around when the bullet struck him. He stumbled back against the front of the adobe, came forward drawing, bringing up his Colt, then half turned, falling against the adobe as Treat fired again and the second bullet hit him.

The revolver fell from Pyke's hand and he stood against the wall staring at Treat, holding his arms bent slightly, but stiffly against his sides, as if afraid to move them. He had been shot through both arms, both just above the elbow.

Treat walked toward him. "Leo," he said, "you've got two things to remember. One, you're not coming back here again. And two, I could've aimed dead center." He turned from Pyke to Sandal. "If you want to do him a good turn, tie up his arms and take him to a doctor. The rest of you," he said to the mounted men, "can tell Mr. Kergosen I'm still here."

★ ★ ★

HE WAS TOLD, and he came the next morning, riding into the yard with a shotgun across his lap. He rode up to Treat, who was standing in front of the adobe, and the shotgun was pointing down at him when Kergosen drew in the reins. They looked at each other in the clear morning sunlight, in the yellow, bright stillness of the yard.

"I could pull the trigger," Kergosen said, "and it would be over."

"Over for me," Treat said. "Not for you or Ellis."

Kergosen sat heavily in the saddle. He had not shaved this morning and his eyes told that he'd had little sleep. "You won't draw a gun against me?"

"No, sir."

"Why?"

"If I did, I'd have to live with Ellis the rest of my life the way you're doing now."

"So you're in a hole."

"But no deeper than the one you're in."

Kergosen studied him. "I underestimated you. I thought you'd run."

"Because you told me to?"

"That was reason enough."

"You're too used to giving orders," Treat said. "You've been Number One a long time and you've forgotten what it's like to have somebody contrary to you."

"I didn't get where I am having people contrary to me," Kergosen stated. "I worked and fought and earned the right to give orders, but I prayed to God to lead me right, and don't you forget that!"

"Mr. Kergosen," Treat said quietly, "are you afraid I can't provide for your daughter?"

"Provide!" Kergosen's face tightened. "An Apache buck provides. He builds a hut for his woman and brings her meat. Any man with one hand and a gun can provide. We're talking about my daughter, not a flat-nosed Indian woman—and you have to put up a damn sight more than meat and a hut!"

Treat said, "You think I won't make something of myself?"

"Mister, all you've proved to me is that you can read sign and shoot." Kergosen paused before asking, "Why didn't you sign a complaint to get Ellis back? Don't you know your rights? That what I'm talking about. You can track a renegade Apache, you can stand off five men with a Colt, but you don't know how to live with a white man!"

"Mr. Kergosen," Treat said patiently, "I could've got a writ. I could've prosecuted you for tearing down my house. I could've killed Leo Pyke with almost a clear conscience. I could've done a lot of things."

"But you didn't," Kergosen said.

"No, I waited."

"If you're waiting for me to die of old age—"

"Mr. Kergosen, I'm interested in your daughter, not your property. We can get along just fine with what we're building on."

"Which is nothing," Kergosen said.

"When you started," Treat asked, "what did you have?"

"When I married I had over one hundred square miles of land. Miles, mister, not acres. I was going on forty years old, sure of myself and not a kid anymore."

"I'm almost thirty, Mr. Kergosen."

"I'll say it again: And you've got nothing."

"Nothing but time."

"Listen," Kergosen said earnestly. "You don't

count on the future like it's nothing but years to fill
up. You fill them up, good or bad, according to
your ability and willingness to sweat, but you're
sure of that future before you ask a woman to face
it with you."

Treat said, "You had somebody picked for Ellis?"

"Not by name, but a man who can offer her
something."

"So you planned her future, and it turned out
different."

"Damn it, I try to do what's right!"

"According to your rules."

"With God's help!"

"Mr. Kergosen," Treat said, "I don't mean disrespect, but I think you've rigged it so God has to
take the blame for your mistakes. Ellis and I made a
mistake. We admit it. We should've come to you
first. We would've got married whether you said yes
or no, but we still should've come to you first. The
way it is now, it's still up to you, but now you're in
an embarrassing position with the Almighty. Ellis
and I are married in the eyes of the same God that
you say's been guiding you all this time, thirty years
or more. All right, you and Him have been getting
along fine up to now. But now what?"

Kergosen said nothing.

"We could probably argue all day," Treat said,

"but it comes down to this: You either go home and send out some more men, or you use that scatter-gun, or you come inside and have some coffee, and we'll talk it over like two grown-up men."

Kergosen stared at him. "I admire your control, Mr. Treat."

"I've learned how to wait, Mr. Kergosen. If it comes down to that, I'll outwait you. I think you know that."

Kergosen was silent for a long moment. He looked down at his hands on the shotgun and ex-haled, letting his breath out slowly, wearily, and he seemed to sit lower on the saddle.

"I think I'm getting old," he said quietly. "I'm tired of arguing and tired of fighting."

"Maybe tired of fighting yourself," Treat said.

Kergosen nodded faintly. "Maybe so."

Treat waited, then said, "Mr. Kergosen, I'm anx-ious to see my wife."

Kergosen's face came up, out of shadow, deep-lined and solemn, but the hard tightness was gone from his jaw. He shifted his weight and came down off the saddle, and on the ground he handed the shotgun to Treat.

"Phil," he said, "this damn thing's getting too heavy to hold."

From his pocket Treat brought out the bank

draft Kergosen had given him. He handed it over, saying, "So is this, Mr. Kergosen."

They stood for a moment. Kergosen's hand went into his pocket with the bank draft and when they moved toward the adobe, the bitterness between them was past. It had worn itself to nothing.

The Nagual

OFELIO OSO—WHO had been a vaquero most of his seventy years, but who now mended fences and drove a wagon for John Stam—looked down the slope through the jack pines seeing the man with his arms about the woman. They were in front of the shack which stood near the edge of the deep ravine bordering the west end of the meadow; and now Ofelio watched them separate lingeringly, the woman moving off, looking back as she passed the corral, going diagonally across the pasture to the trees on the far side, where she disappeared.

Now Mrs. Stam goes home, Ofelio thought, to wait for her husband.

The old man had seen them like this before, sometimes in the evening, sometimes at dawn as it was now with the first distant sun streak off beyond the Organ Mountains, and always when John Stam was away. This had been going on for months now, at least since Ofelio first began going up into the hills at night.

It was a strange feeling that caused the old man to do this; more an urgency, for he had come to a realization that there was little time left for him. In the hills at night a man can think clearly, and when a man believes his end is approaching there are things to think about.

In his sixty-ninth year Ofelio Oso broke his leg. In the shock of a pain-stabbing moment it was smashed between horse and corral post as John Stam's cattle rushed the gate opening. He could no longer ride, after having done nothing else for more than fifty years; and with this came the certainty that his end was approaching. Since he was of no use to anyone, then only death remained. In his idleness he could feel its nearness and he thought of many things to prepare himself for the day it would come.

Now he waited until the horsebreaker, Joe Slidell, went into the shack. Ofelio limped down the slope through the pines and was crossing a corner of the pasture when Joe Slidell reappeared, leaning in the doorway with something in his hand, looking absently out at the few mustangs off at the far end of the pasture. His gaze moved to the bay stallion in the corral, then swung slowly until he was looking at Ofelio Oso.

The old man saw this and changed his direction, going toward the shack. He carried a blanket over his shoulder and wore a willow-root Chihuahua hat, and his hand touched the brim of it as he approached the loose figure in the doorway.

"At it again," Joe Slidell said. He lifted the bottle which he held close to his stomach and took a good drink. Then he lowered it, and his face contorted. He grunted, "Yaaaaa!" but after that he seemed relieved. He nodded to the hill and said, "How long you been up there?"

"Through the night," Ofelio answered. Which you well know, he thought. You, standing there drinking the whiskey that the woman brings.

Slidell wiped his mouth with the back of his hand, watching the old man through heavy-lidded eyes. "What do you see up there?"

"Many things."

"Like what?"

Ofelio shrugged. "I have seen devils."

Slidell grinned. "Big ones or little ones?"

"They take many forms."

Joe Slidell took another drink of the whiskey, not offering it to the old man, then said, "Well, I got work to do." He nodded to the corral where the bay stood looking over the rail, lifting and shaking his maned head at the man smell. "That horse," Joe Slidell said, "is going to finish gettin' himself broke today, one way or the other."

Ofelio looked at the stallion admiringly. A fine animal for long rides, for the killing pace, but for cutting stock, no. It would never be trained to swerve inward and break into a dead run at the feel of boot touching stirrup. He said to the horse-breaker, "That bay is much horse."

"Close to seventeen hands," Joe Slidell said, "if you was to get close enough to measure."

"This is the one for Señor Stam's use?"

Slidell nodded. "Maybe. If I don't ride him down to the house before supper, you bring up a mule to haul his carcass to the ravine." He jerked his thumb past his head, indicating the deep draw behind the shack. Ofelio had been made to do this before. The mule dragged the still faintly breathing mustang to the ravine edge. Then Slidell would tell him to push, while he levered with a pole, until finally the mustang went over the side down the steep-slanted seventy feet to the bottom.

★   ★   ★

OFELIO CROSSED the pasture, then down into the woods that fell gradually for almost a mile before opening again at the house and out-buildings of John Stam's spread. That *jinete*—that breaker of horses—is very sure of himself, the old man thought, moving through the trees. Both with horses and another man's wife. He must know I have seen them together, but it doesn't bother him. No, the old man thought now, it is something other than being sure of himself. I think it is stupidity. An intelligent man tames a wild horse with a great deal of respect, for he knows the horse is able to kill him. As for Mrs. Stam, considering her husband, one would think he would treat her with even greater respect.

Marion Stam was on the back porch while Ofelio hitched the mules to the flatbed wagon. Her arms were folded across her chest and she watched the old man because his hitching the team was the only activity in the yard. Marion Stam's eyes were listless, darkly shadowed, making her thin face seem transparently frail, and this made her look older than her twenty-five years. But appearance made little difference to Marion. John Stam was nearly twice her age; and Joe Slidell—Joe spent all his time up at the horse camp, anything in a dress looked good to him.

But the boredom. This was the only thing to which Marion Stam could not resign herself. A house miles away from nowhere. Day following day, each one utterly void of anything resembling her estimation of living. John Stam at the table, eyes on his plate, opening his mouth only to put food into it. The picture of John Stam at night, just before blowing out the lamp, standing in his yellowish, musty-smelling long underwear. "Good night," a grunt, then the sound of even, open-mouthed breathing. Joe Slidell relieved some of the boredom. Some. He was young, not bad looking in a coarse way, but, Lord, he smelled like one of his horses!

"Why're you going now?" she called to Ofelio. "The stage's always late."

The old man looked up. "Someday it will be early. Perhaps this morning."

The woman shrugged, leaning in the door frame now, her arms still folded over her thin chest as Ofelio moved the team and wagon creaking out of the yard.

But the stage was not early; nor was it on time. Ofelio urged the mules into the empty station yard and pulled to a slow stop in front of the wagon shed that joined the station adobe. Two horses were in the shed with their muzzles munching at the hay rack. Spainhower, the Butterfield agent, appeared in the doorway for a moment. Seeing Ofelio he said, "Seems you'd learn to leave about thirty minutes later." He turned away.

Ofelio smiled, climbing off the wagon box. He went through the door, following Spainhower into the sudden dimness, feeling the adobe still cool from the night and hearing a voice saying: "If Ofelio drove for Butterfield, nobody'd have to wait for stages." He recognized the voice and the soft laugh that followed and then he saw the man, Billy-Jack Trew, sitting on one end of the pine table with his boots resting on a Douglas chair.

Billy-Jack Trew was a deputy. Val Dodson, his boss, the Doña Ana sheriff, sat a seat away from him with his elbows on the pine boards. They had come down from Tularosa, stopping for a drink before going on to Mesilla.

Billy-Jack Trew said in Spanish, "Ofelio, how does it go?"

The old man nodded. "It passes well," he said, and smiled, because Billy-Jack was a man you smiled at even though you knew him slightly and saw him less than once in a month.

"Up there at that horse pasture," the deputy said, "I hear Joe Slidell's got some mounts of his own."

Ofelio nodded. "I think so. Señor Stam does not own all of them."

"I'm going to take me a ride up there pretty soon," Billy-Jack said, "and see what kind of money Joe's askin'. Way the sheriff keeps me going I need two horses, and that's a fact."

Ofelio could feel Spainhower looking at him, Val Dodson glancing now and then. One or the other would soon ask about his nights in the hills. He could feel this also. Everyone seemed to know about his going into the hills and everyone continued to question him about it, as if it were a foolish thing to do. Only Billy-Jack Trew would talk about it seriously.

★ ★ ★

AT FIRST, OFELIO had tried to explain the things he thought about: life and death and a man's place, the temptations of the devil and man's obligation to God—all those things men begin to think about when there is little time left. And from the beginning Ofelio saw that they were laughing at him. Serious faces straining to hold back smiles.

Pseudosincere questions that were only to lead him on. So after the first few times he stopped telling them what occurred to him in the loneliness of the night and would tell them whatever entered his mind, though much of it was still fact.

Billy-Jack Trew listened, and in a way he understood the old man. He knew that legends were part of a Mexican peon's life. He knew that Ofelio had been a vaquero for something like fifty years, with lots of lonesome time for imagining things. Anything the old man said was good listening, and a lot of it made sense after you thought about it awhile—so Billy-Jack Trew didn't laugh.

With a cigar stub clamped in the corner of his mouth, Spainhower's puffy face was dead serious looking at the old man. "Ofelio," he said, "this morning there was a mist ring over the gate. Now, I heard what that meant, so I kept my eyes open and sure'n hell here come a gang of elves through the gate dancin' and carryin' on. They marched right in here and hauled themselves up on that table."

Val Dodson said dryly, "Now, that's funny, just this morning coming down from Tularosa me and Billy-Jack looked up to see this be-ootiful she-devil running like hell for a cholla clump." He paused, glancing at Ofelio. "Billy-Jack took one look and was half out his saddle when I grabbed him."

Billy-Jack Trew shook his head. "Ofelio, don't mind that talk."

The old man smiled, saying nothing.

"You seen any more devils?" Spainhower asked him.

Ofelio hesitated, then nodded, saying, "Yes, I saw two devils this morning. Just at dawn."

Spainhower said, "What'd they look like?"

"I know," Val Dodson said quickly.

"Aw, Val," Billy-Jack said. "Leave him alone." He glanced at Ofelio, who was looking at Dodson intently, as if afraid of what he would say next.

"I'll bet," Dodson went on, "they had horns and hairy forked tails like that one me and Billy-Jack saw out on the sands." Spainhower laughed, then Dodson winked at him and laughed too.

*   *   *

BILLY-JACK TREW WAS watching Ofelio and he saw the tense expression on the old man's face relax. He saw the half-frightened look change to a smile of relief, and Billy-Jack was thinking that maybe a man ought to listen even a little closer to what Ofelio said. Like maybe there were double meanings to the things he said.

"Listen," Ofelio said, "I will tell you something else I have seen. A sight few men have ever witnessed." Ofelio was thinking: All right, give them something for their minds to work on.

"What I saw is a very hideous thing to behold, more frightening than elves, more terrible than devils." He paused, then said quietly, "What I saw was a *nagual*."

He waited, certain they had never heard of this, for it was an old Mexican legend. Spainhower was smiling, but half-squinting curiosity was in his eyes. Dodson was watching, waiting for him to go on. Still Ofelio hesitated and finally Spainhower said, "And what's a *nagual* supposed to be?"

"A *nagual*," Ofelio explained carefully, "is a man with strange powers. A man who is able to transform himself into a certain animal."

Spainhower said, too quickly, "What kind of an animal?"

"That," Ofelio answered, "depends upon the man. The animal is usually of his choice."

Spainhower's brow was deep furrowed. "What's so terrible about that?"

Ofelio's face was serious. "One can see you have never beheld a *nagual*. Tell me, what is more hideous, what is more terrible, than a man—who is made in God's image—becoming an animal?"

There was silence. Then Val Dodson said, "Aw—"

Spainhower didn't know what to say; he felt disappointed, cheated.

And into this silence came the faint rumbling sound. Billy-Jack Trew said, "Here she comes." They stood up, moving for the door, and soon the rumble was higher pitched—creaking, screeching, rattling, pounding—and the Butterfield stage was swinging into the yard. Spainhower and Dodson and Billy-Jack Trew went outside, Ofelio and his *nagual* forgotten.

No one had ever seen John Stam smile. Some, smiling themselves, said Marion must have at least once or twice, but most doubted even this. John Stam worked hard, twelve to sixteen hours a day, plus keeping a close eye on some business interests he had in Mesilla, and had been doing it since he'd first visually staked off his range six years before. No one asked where he came from and John Stam didn't volunteer any answers.

Billy-Jack Trew said Stam looked to him like a red-dirt farmer with no business in cattle, but that was once Billy-Jack was wrong and he admitted it himself later. John Stam appeared one day with a crow-bait horse and twelve mavericks including a bull. Now, six years later, he had himself way over a thousand head and a *jinete* to break him all the horses he could ride.

Off the range, though, he let Ofelio Oso drive
him wherever he went. Some said he felt sorry for
Ofelio because the old Mexican had been a good
hand in his day. Others said Marion put him up to
it so she wouldn't have Ofelio hanging around the
place all the time. There was always some talk
about Marion, especially now with the cut-down
crew up at the summer range, John Stam gone to
tend his business about once a week, and only Ofelio and Joe Slidell there. Joe Slidell wasn't a bad-
looking man.

The first five years John Stam allowed himself
only two pleasures: he drank whiskey, though no
one had ever seen him drinking it, only buying it;
and every Sunday afternoon he'd ride to Mesilla for
dinner at the hotel. He would always order the
same thing, chicken, and always sit at the same
table. He had been doing this for some time when
Marion started waiting tables there. Two years
later, John Stam asked her to marry him as she was
setting down his dessert and Marion said yes then
and there. Some claimed the only thing he'd said to
her before that was bring me the ketchup.

Spainhower said it looked to him like Stam was
from a line of hardheaded Dutchmen. Probably his
dad had made him work like a mule and never told
him about women, Spainhower said, so John Stam

never knew what it was like *not* to work and the first woman he looked up long enough to notice, he married. About everybody agreed Spainhower had something.

They were almost to the ranch before John Stam spoke. He had nodded to the men in the station yard, but gotten right up on the wagon seat. Spainhower asked him if he cared for a drink, but he shook his head. When they were in view of the ranch house—John Stam's leathery mask of a face looking straight ahead down the slope—he said, "Mrs. Stam is in the house?"

"I think so," Ofelio said, looking at him quickly, then back to the rumps of the mules.

"All morning?"

"I was not here all morning." Ofelio waited, but John Stam said no more. This was the first time Ofelio had been questioned about Mrs. Stam. Perhaps he overheard talk in Mesilla, he thought.

★ ★ ★

IN THE YARD John Stam climbed off the wagon and went into the house. Ofelio headed the team for the barn and stopped before the wide door to unhitch. The yard was quiet; he glanced at the house, which seemed deserted, though he knew John Stam was inside. Suddenly Mrs. Stam's voice was coming from the house, high pitched, excited, the words not clear. The sound stopped abruptly and it was quiet again. A few minutes later the screen door slammed and John Stam was coming across the yard, his great gnarled hands hanging empty, threateningly, at his sides.

He stopped before Ofelio and said bluntly, "I'm asking you if you've ever taken any of my whiskey."

"I have never tasted whiskey," Ofelio said and felt a strange guilt come over him in this man's gaze. He tried to smile. "But in the past I've tasted enough mescal to make up for it."

John Stam's gaze held. "That wasn't what I asked you."

"All right," Ofelio said. "I have never taken any."

"I'll ask you once more," John Stam said.

Ofelio was bewildered. "What would you have me say?"

For a long moment John Stam stared. His eyes were hard though there was a weariness in them. He said, "I don't need you around here, you know."

"I have told the truth," Ofelio said simply.

The rancher continued to stare, a muscle in his cheek tightening and untightening. He turned abruptly and went back to the house.

The old man thought of the times he had seen Joe Slidell and the woman together and the times he had seen Joe Slidell drinking the whiskey she brought to him. Ofelio thought: He wasn't asking about whiskey, he was asking about his wife. But he could not come out with it. He knows something is going on behind his back, or else he suspicions it strongly, and he sees a relation between it and the whiskey that's being taken. I think I feel sorry for him; he hasn't learned to keep his woman and he doesn't know what to do.

Before supper Joe Slidell came down out of the woods trail on the bay stallion. He dismounted at the back porch and he and John Stam talked for a few minutes looking over the horse. When Joe Slidell left, John Stam, holding the bridle, watched him disappear into the woods and for a long time after, he stood there staring at the trail that went up through the woods.

Just before dark John Stam rode out of the yard on the bay stallion. Later—it was full dark then—Ofelio heard the screen door again. He rose from his bunk in the end barn stall and opened the big door an inch, in time to see Marion Stam's dim form pass into the trees.

He has left, Ofelio thought, so she goes to the *jinete*. He shook his head thinking: This is none of your business. But it remained in his mind and later, with his blanket over his shoulder, he went into the hills where he could think of these things more clearly.

He moved through the woods hearing the night sounds which seemed far away and his own footsteps in the leaves that were close, but did not seem to belong to him; then he was on the pine slope and high up he felt the breeze. For a time he listened to the soft sound of it in the jack pines. Tomorrow there will be rain, he thought. Sometime in the afternoon.

He stretched out on the ground, rolling the blanket behind his head, and looked up at the dim stars thinking: More and more every day, *viejo,* you must realize you are no longer of any value. The horsebreaker is not afraid of you, the men at the station laugh and take nothing you say seriously, and finally Señor Stam, he made it very clear when he said, "I don't need you around here."

Then why does he keep me—months now since I have been dismounted—except out of charity? He is a strange man. I suppose I owe him something, something more than feeling sorry for him which does him no good. I think we have something in common. I can feel sorry for both of us. He laughed at this and tried to discover other things they might have in common. It relaxed him, his imagination wandering, and soon he dozed off with the cool breeze on his face, not remembering to think about his end approaching.

★ ★ ★

To THE EAST, above the chimneys of the Organ range, morning light began to gray-streak the day. Ofelio opened his eyes, hearing the horse moving through the trees below him: hooves clicking the small stones and the swish of pine branches. He thought of Joe Slidell's mustangs. One of them has wandered up the slope. But then, the unmistakable squeak of saddle leather and he sat up, tensed. It could be anyone, he thought. Almost anyone.

He rose, folding the blanket over his shoulder, and made his way down the slope silently, following the sound of the horse, and when he reached the pasture he saw the dim shape of it moving toward the shack, a tall shadow gliding away from him in the half light.

The door opened. Joe Slidell came out, closing it quickly behind him. "You're up early," he said, yawning, pulling a suspender over his shoulder. "How's that horse carry you? He learned his manners yesterday . . . won't give you no trouble. If he does, you let me have him back for about an hour."

Slidell looked above the horse to the rider. "Mr. Stam, why're you lookin' at me like that?" He squinted up in the dimness. "Mr. Stam, what's the matter? You feelin' all right?"

"Tell her to come out," John Stam said.

"What?"

"I said tell her to come out."

"Now, Mr. Stam—" Slidell's voice trailed off, but slowly a grin formed on his mouth. He said, almost embarrassedly, "Well, Mr. Stam, I didn't think you'd mind." One man talking to another now. "Hell, it's only a little Mex gal from Mesilla. It gets lonely here and—"

John Stam spurred the stallion violently; the great stallion lunged, rearing, coming down with thrashing hooves on the screaming man. Slidell went down covering his head, falling against the shack boards. He clung there gasping as the stallion backed off; the next moment he was crawling frantically, rising, stumbling, running; he looked back seeing John Stam spurring and he screamed again as the stallion ran him down. John Stam reined in a tight circle and came back over the motionless form. He dismounted before the shack and went inside.

Go away, quickly, Ofelio told himself, and started for the other side of the pasture, running tensed, not wanting to hear what he knew would come. But he could not outrun it, the scream came turning him around when he was almost to the woods.

Marion Stam was in the doorway, then running across the yard, swerving as she saw the corral suddenly in front of her. John Stam was in the saddle spurring the stallion after her, gaining as she followed the rail circle of the corral. Now she was looking back, seeing the stallion almost on top of her. The stallion swerved suddenly as the woman screamed going over the edge of the ravine.

Ofelio ran to the trees before looking back. John Stam had dismounted. He removed bridle and saddle from the bay and put these in the shack. Then he picked up a stone and threw it at the stallion, sending it galloping for the open pasture.

The old man was breathing in short gasps from the running, but he hurried now through the woods and did not stop until he reached the barn. He sat on the bunk listening to his heart, feeling it in his chest. Minutes later John Stam opened the big door. He stood looking down at Ofelio while the old man's mind repeated: Mary, Virgin and Mother, until he heard the rancher say, "You didn't see or hear anything all night. I didn't leave the house, did I?"

Ofelio hesitated, then nodded slowly as if committing this to memory. "You did not leave the house."

John Stam's eyes held threateningly before he turned and went out. Minutes later Ofelio saw him leave the house with a shotgun under his arm. He crossed the yard and entered the woods. Already he is unsure, Ofelio thought, especially of the woman, though the fall was at least seventy feet.

* * *

WHEN HE HEARD the horse come down out of the woods it was barely more than an hour later. Ofelio looked out, expecting to see John Stam on the bay, but it was Billy-Jack Trew walking his horse into the yard. Quickly the old man climbed the ladder to the loft. The deputy went to the house first and called out. When there was no answer he approached the barn and called Ofelio's name.

He's found them! But what brought him? Ah, the old man thought, remembering, he wants to buy a horse. He spoke of that yesterday. But he found them instead. Where is Señor Stam? Why didn't he see him? He heard the deputy call again, but still Ofelio did not come out. He remained crouched in the darkness of the barn loft until he heard the deputy leave.

The door opened and John Stam stood below in the strip of outside light.

Resignedly, Ofelio said, "I am here," looking down, thinking: He was close all the time. He followed the deputy back and if I had called he would have killed both of us. And he is very capable of killing.

John Stam looked up, studying the old man. Finally he said, "You were there last night; I'm sure of it now . . . else you wouldn't be hiding, afraid of admitting something. You were smart not to talk to him. Maybe you're remembering you owe me something for keeping you on, even though you're not good for anything." He added abruptly, "You believe in God?"

Ofelio nodded.

"Then," John Stam said, "swear to God you'll never mention my name in connection with what happened."

Ofelio nodded again, resignedly, thinking of his obligation to this man. "I swear it," he said.

The rain came in the late afternoon, keeping Ofelio inside the barn. He crouched in the doorway, listening to the soft hissing of the rain in the trees, watching the puddles forming in the wagon tracks. His eyes would go to the house, picturing John Stam inside alone with his thoughts and waiting. They will come. Perhaps the rain will delay them, Ofelio thought, but they will come.

The sheriff will say, Mr. Stam this is a terrible thing we have to tell you. What? Well, you know the stallion Joe Slidell was breaking? Well, it must have got loose. It looks like Joe tried to catch him and . . . Joe got under his hooves. And, Mrs. Stam was there . . . we figured she was up to look at your new horse—saying this with embarrassment. She must have become frightened when it happened and she ran. In the dark she went over the side of the ravine. Billy-Jack found them this morning. . . .

He did not hear them because of the rain. He was staring at a puddle and when he looked up there was Val Dodson and Billy-Jack Trew. It was too late to climb to the loft.

Billy-Jack smiled. "I was around earlier, but I didn't see you." His hat was low, shielding his face from the light rain, as was Dodson's.

Ofelio could feel himself trembling. He is watching now from a window. Mother of God, help me.

Dodson said, "Where's Stam?"

Ofelio hesitated, then nodded toward the house.

"Come on," Dodson said. "Let's get it over with."

Billy-Jack Trew leaned closer, resting his forearm

on the saddle horn. He said gently, "Have you seen anything more since yesterday?"

Ofelio looked up, seeing the wet smiling face and another image that was in his mind—a great stallion in the dawn light—and the words came out suddenly, as if forced from his mouth. He said, "I saw a *nagual*!"

Dodson groaned. "Not again," and nudged his horse with his knees.

"Wait a minute," Billy-Jack said quickly. Then to Ofelio, "This *nagual*, you actually saw it?"

The old man bit his lips. "Yes."

"It was an animal you saw, then."

"It was a *nagual*."

Dodson said, "You stand in the rain and talk crazy. I'm getting this over with."

Billy-Jack swung down next to the old man. "Listen a minute, Val." To Ofelio, gently again, "But it was in the form of an animal?"

Ofelio's head nodded slowly.

"What did the animal look like?"

"It was," the old man said slowly, not looking at the deputy, "a great stallion." He said quickly, "I can tell you no more than that."

Dodson dismounted.

Billy-Jack said, "And where did the *nagual* go?"

Ofelio was looking beyond the deputy toward the house. He saw the back door open and John Stam came out on the porch, the shotgun cradled in his arm. Ofelio continued to stare. He could not speak as it went through his mind: He thinks I have told them!

Seeing the old man's face, Billy-Jack turned, then Dodson.

Stam called, "Ofelio, come here!"

Billy-Jack said, "Stay where you are," and now his voice was not gentle. But the hint of a smile returned as he unfastened the two lower buttons of his slicker and suddenly he called, "Mr. Stam! You know what a *nagual* is?" He opened the slicker all the way and drew a tobacco plug from his pants pocket.

Dodson whispered hoarsely, "What's the matter with you!"

Billy-Jack was smiling. "I'm only askin' a simple question."

John Stam did not answer. He was staring at Ofelio.

"Mr. Stam," Billy-Jack Trew called, "before I tell you what a *nagual* is I want to warn you I can get out a Colt a helluva lot quicker than you can swing a shotgun."

* * *

OFELIO OSO DIED at the age of ninety-three on a ranch outside Tularosa. They said about him he sure told some tall ones—about devils, and about seeing a *nagual* hanged for murder in Mesilla . . . whatever that meant . . . but he was much man. Even at his age the old son relied on no one, wouldn't let a soul do anything for him, and died owing the world not one plugged peso. And wasn't the least bit afraid to die, even though he was so old. He used to say, "Listen, if there is no way to tell when death will come, then why should one be afraid of it?"

The stories contained in this volume originally appeared in the following publications:

"Law of the Hunted Ones," *Western Story Magazine*, December 1952

"The Hard Way," *Zane Grey's Western*, August 1953

"Trouble at Rindo's Station," *Argosy*, October 1953

"No Man's Guns," *Western Story Roundup*, August 1955

"The Rancher's Lady," *Western Magazine*, September 1955

"Moment of Vengeance," *Saturday Evening Post*, April 21, 1956

"The Nagual," *2-Gun Western*, November 1956